THE INVINCIBLE SHOVEL

NOVEL 1

"WAVE MOTION SHOVEL BLAST!"
(´・ω・)σ===★('Д')・∴ KA-CHOOOM

W9-ADL-202

📖 GLOSSARY 1

Shovel

noun

① Beam Weapon. Acts as a Wave Motion Shovel Blast when heated.

② Refers to a god or something even more divine.

③ A tool that is largely used for shoveling. (Rarely used for this purpose.)

adjective

① Strong, dependable, manly, attractive.

② A condition that the ladies adore, or those actions.

③ Extremely lovely.

verb

① Something far too embarrassing to write here. Please refer to page 58.

HOLY SHOVEL EMPIRE, OFFICIAL DICTIONARY
(AUTHOR: LITHISIA), 7TH VERSION.

Lithisia

SHOVEL PRINCESS
HEIR TO ROSTIR THRONE

"This is a shovel...?"

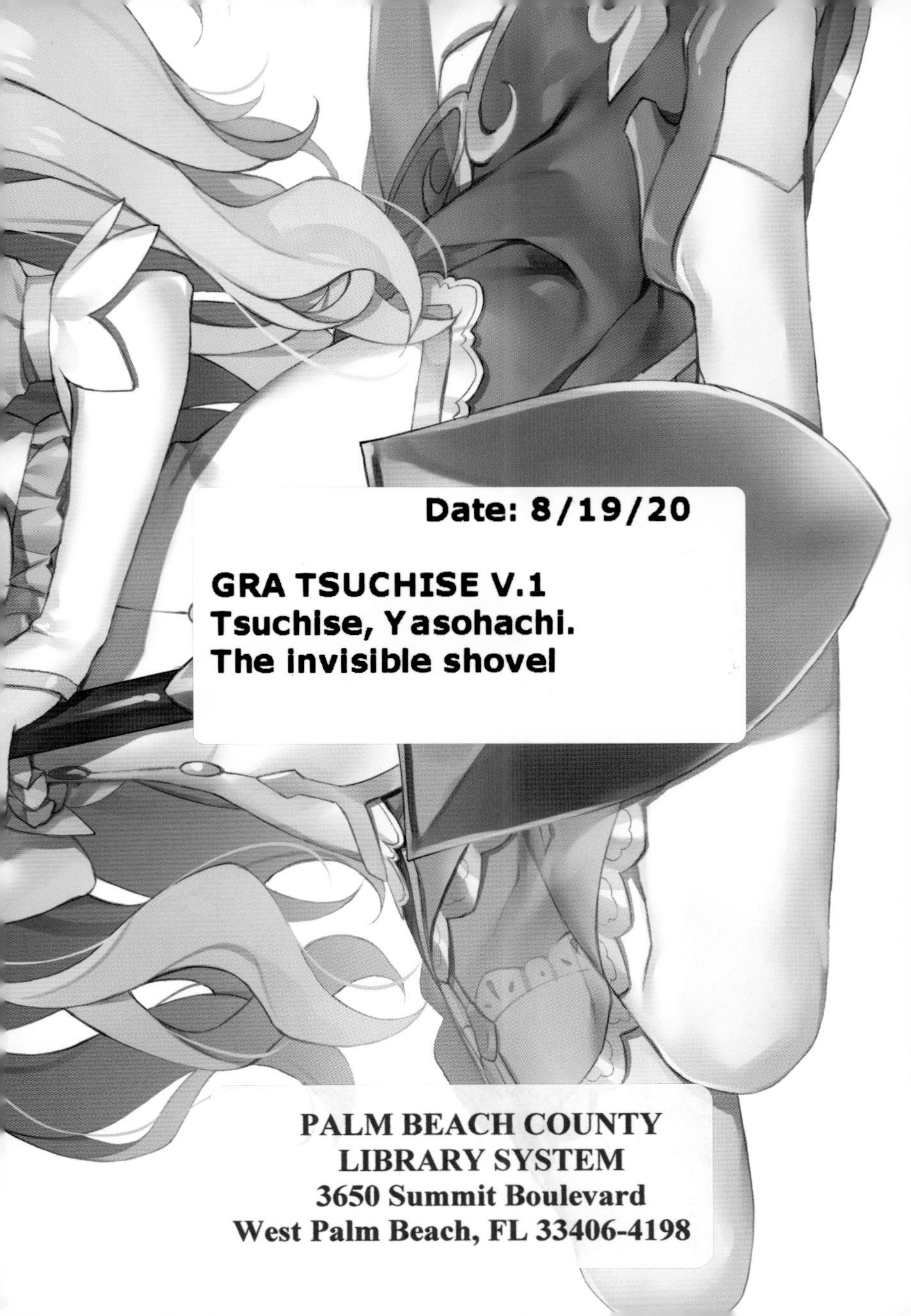

"Um, um! I–Is this really the right way to hold it?!"

WELL–ENDOWED ELF
Fiorie!

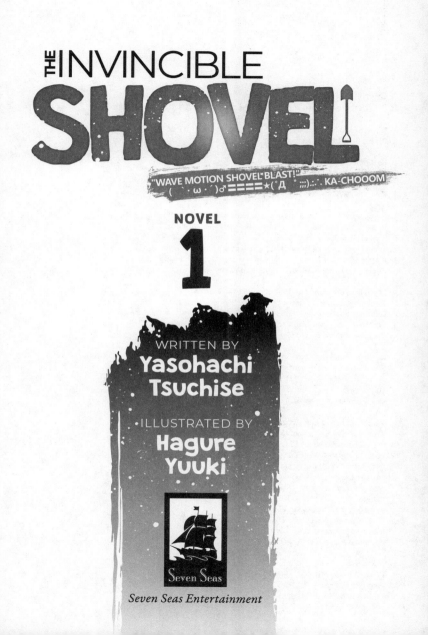

THE INVINCIBLE SHOVEL

"WAVE MOTION SHOVEL BLAST!"
(・ω・)σ ===== ★(°Д °;;;) KA-CHOOOM

NOVEL 1

WRITTEN BY
Yasohachi Tsuchise

ILLUSTRATED BY
Hagure Yuuki

Seven Seas

Seven Seas Entertainment

SCOOP MUSO
　「SCOOP HADOHO!」 (｀・ω・´)♂=====★(°Д° ;;;).:. DOGOoo

©Yasohachi Tsuchise 2019
Illustrations by Hagure Yuuki

First published in Japan in 2019 by
KADOKAWA CORPORATION, Tokyo.
English translation rights arranged with
KADOKAWA CORPORATION, Tokyo.

Seven Seas press and purchase enquiries can be sent to
Marketing Manager Lianne Sentar at press@gomanga.com.
Information requiring the distribution and purchase of
digital editions is available from Digital Manager CK Russell
at digital@gomanga.com.

Seven Seas and the Seven Seas logo are trademarks of
Seven Seas Entertainment. All rights reserved.

Follow Seven Seas Entertainment online at
sevenseasentertainment.com.

TRANSLATION: Elliot Ryoga
ADAPTATION: Renee Baumgartner
COVER DESIGN: Nicky Lim
LOGO DESIGN: George Panella
INTERIOR LAYOUT & DESIGN: Clay Gardner
PROOFREADER: Kelly Lorraine Andrews, Stephanie Cohen
LIGHT NOVEL EDITOR: Nibedita Sen
PREPRESS TECHNICIAN: Rhiannon Rasmussen-Silverstein
PRODUCTION MANAGER: Lissa Pattillo
MANAGING EDITOR: Julie Davis
ASSOCIATE PUBLISHER: Adam Arnold
PUBLISHER: Jason DeAngelis

ISBN: 978-1-64505-442-9
Printed in Canada
First Printing: May 2020
10 9 8 7 6 5 4 3 2 1

CONTENTS

PROLOGUE
The Strongest Miner on the Surface

THE FIRST TIME Alan's shovel fired a beam, he'd been working as a miner for a hundred years.

"Uh..." He stood there, surveying the damage. "Can't say I've ever seen a shovel do *that* before..."

Apparently, this particular shovel did a lot more than turn the earth. At the very least, it could fire an absolutely devastating beam of light.

"Well," Alan said after the dust settled. "Might as well put this thing to the test..."

He turned to a boulder situated nearby. BLAM! The shovel erupted with blue energy, digging a furrow several inches deep into the stone. He'd heard of a spell like this before: "Energy Bolt" or something like that. Alan wasn't exactly the sharpest tool in the shed (even if his shovel was now a candidate for the title), so he resolved to call this power the "Shovel Bolt."

"That's well and good," he said, "But I can't see how this is going to help me dig up any jewels..."

And so he returned to work, putting all thought of the curious shovel behind him.

⊳━━━━▶

Prospecting for jewels was Alan's specialty, and in all the land, no one was his equal in the trade. The gems he found weren't just sparkling rocks, either; they were fuel for powerful magical artifacts.

Day in and day out, he toiled underneath a mountain out in the country, working the earth he'd inherited from his father. Out there on the edge of the land, he pretty much never saw visitors. Every few years or so, somebody from the Mages' Guild in the capital would swing by to buy the jewels Alan had found. It was easy to make ends meet like that. Apparently, he was kind of famous back in town; they called him "the Old Digger."

It was a simple life, but Alan enjoyed it. Mining for baubles was a fun job.

There was just one problem.

"I gotta find me an apprentice..."

A measure of dwarven blood ran in Alan's veins. Thanks to his peculiar ancestry, he could expect to live a hundred and fifty years, but he'd already seen a hundred and twenty of those pass him by. It wouldn't be long before his stamina started to wane. He figured that once he noticed going up and down the mountain's three thousand steps starting to become a chore, it'd be time to go hunting for a successor.

But hundreds of years passed, and the steps never got any harder. Eventually, even Alan couldn't help but find that a little odd.

"Hrrrm."

Despite living multiple times his natural lifespan, he kept on going the same as he always had, his energy never flagging.

"It's peculiar," he said at last. "Passing strange, even."

Alan didn't grow old. If anything, he only grew stronger. His muscles became so chiseled it was like he was carved from the mountain himself. He could do 10,000 squat jumps up and down the stairs cut into the mountain without shedding a single drop of sweat.

"Sir Digger, you look even younger than you did last year! I'm so glad you're in good health," said the visitor from the Mages' Guild.

Something wasn't right.

It was then that Alan recalled the moment long ago when he'd fired a beam from his shovel. If his calculations were correct, that was the precise instant he'd stopped aging.

Alan had to test his theory. He lifted his shovel and once again tried firing a beam.

KA-CHOOOOOOOOOOOM!!!!

A thick beam of light about three feet in diameter annihilated a nearby boulder.

"Whoooooaaaa!" Alan was momentarily stunned by the power he'd just wielded. He stood in shock for a moment before he came to a realization. "I can mine for even *more* jewels with this thing!"

The most valuable gems were hidden deep beneath the surface, where the earth itself was much harder. Fortunately for Alan, he now had the power to melt right through that stony soil. With his amazing shovel in hand, he could mine harder and deeper than ever before. It wasn't long before he forgot about the whole aging thing.

Alan threw himself back into the mining life, his Shovel Bolt growing stronger and stronger as he dug ever deeper into the mountain. The deeper he dug, the more experienced he became with his shovel, and slowly, he gained new abilities.

By the time Alan had made his way down thirty layers of the mountain, he was able to bend his beam. Upon hitting the hundredth layer, he could use his beam like a type of spread shot, allowing him to dig in multiple spots simultaneously. At Layer #256, Alan could create a beam barrier, perfect for protecting against falling rocks and the like.

He dug deeper and deeper. Eventually, Alan came upon a dark shrine, surrounded by lava and guarded by demons. He soon realized he'd dug to the thousandth layer beneath the mountain...what looked to be Hell itself.

"This shrine... It's made of jewels I've never seen before!" shouted Alan in surprise, still a jewel miner to his core.

And so, Alan dug for jewels in Hell. He was attacked by demons time and time again, but he fought them off with his Shovel Bolt. A dragon made an appearance, but even it was no match for the power of Alan and his miraculous shovel. Finally, the Emperor of Hell himself declared war on Alan, sending an army of three hundred demons and thirty ancient dragons after this unwelcome miner. In the centuries to come, this would be referred to as the legendary "Jewel War."

In the end, the Emperor of Hell and his armies were destroyed by the invincible shovel's powers. Alan simply dusted himself off and went back to work. Centuries passed this way, with Alan and his shovel happily mining the earth for shining gems.

But after a thousand years, something happened on the surface.

CHAPTER 1

Shovel on a Journey
(LITHISIA'S INTRODUCTION)

PART 1

The Miner Fires His Beam

IT HAD BEEN SOME TIME since Alan had last descended from the mountain. If he had counted correctly, the last time he'd gone to the surface world was 256 years ago.

"Whew, that's a long time," he said to himself. "I bet nobody remembers me. Heck, there probably isn't anyone alive who would."

After discovering a vein of a special mineral he'd dubbed "Demonite," Alan spent years upon years mining the precious resource. Food and drink weren't a problem; Alan knew how to survive underground for years on end. Hell was just a fancier part of the mine, as far as he was concerned, and he was able to find sustenance.

Thanks to his survivalist skills and unwavering passion for mining, Alan had amassed a large quantity of goods.

The problem was, he didn't know who to sell his wares to. As far as he knew, the Mages' Guild he used to deal with was long gone.

He packed up his wares, along with his trusty shovel, and began to make his way up out of Hell and back down the mountain path. *First things first,* he thought to himself. *I gotta find a market for my goods, and then find a way to train an apprentice to be my successor someday. Wonder if—*

"Aaaaaaaaah!!!!"

His musings were cut off by the screams of what sounded like a young woman.

"Huh!" With his trusty shovel in hand, Alan made haste to the area where the screams were coming from. It was his responsibility to save a woman in need. This was part of what being a miner meant, or so his father had taught him some thousand years ago.

The other thing his old man ingrained in him was to find a wife for himself so he could ensure there would be a successor to the family business. Not that that mattered at the moment.

"Are you all right?! Do you need help?" Alan asked upon arriving at the scene. He surveyed the area. There was a busted carriage in the middle of the road. Not far from it was a young lady surrounded by a group of gruff-looking men. Alan assumed they were bandits or something. They were obviously up to no good.

One of them grabbed the girl by her golden locks while another pulled at her pure white dress. She looked for all the world like a beautiful princess. "Let me go! Please!" the girl cried.

"Oooooooooooh! Ain't you nice and soft, ya fake Princess!"

"Aaaaah! Let goooo!"

"C'mon, you damn idiot. Don't damage the goods. We got a million gold coins riding on her head."

Alan didn't quite follow their conversation, but he could at least tell that the young lady was being attacked by these ruffians, which meant he had only one course of action to take. He stepped forward, brandishing his shovel. "Stop this at once!" he shouted.

"Wha…?" The head of the bandits looked at Alan and his shovel, then tilted his head in confusion. "Who the hell are you, and what's up with that shovel?"

"My name is Alan, and I am a miner. Release the lady at once. If you don't…" He gripped his shovel tightly. "The power of my shovel will render your lives forfeit."

A moment passed in silence. Another heartbeat, two; and then the bandits broke out into hysterical laughter.

"Ahhahahaha! Quit while yer ahead, old man!" one of them said. "The boss here used to be a Holy Knight!"

The boss slapped his knee with mirth. "Ahhaha! 'The power of my shovel will render your lives forfeit'?! Hahaha! What a stupid line! That's a new one on me!" said the leader of the bandits. He squared off against Alan, totally unfazed by his threat. "Look, Mr. Miner. This ain't got nothing to do with you. If you don't wanna die here…"

Swoosh. A flash of light quickly moved through the air, and a crack appeared along the ground beneath Alan. The leader had drawn his longsword and used one of its powers in one smooth motion. "Then just head on home," he finished.

The bandit leader clearly had no intention of backing down. Alan would have to fight. He grimaced, none too pleased about using Shovel Bolt against another human being, but he wasn't about to let these bandits hurt the girl.

Alan gripped his shovel even tighter and concentrated. His eyes narrowed, locking onto his target—the bandit leader's sword.

"Psh," the leader scoffed. "Looks like you're asking for a bruisin'. Hiiyah!" The gruff-looking man swept his sword down toward Alan, expecting this fight to end like all the others. His underlings hadn't lied about him being a former Holy Knight. He was fast, and his swordplay was clean and accurate. Anyone else would have been dead in a second, sliced in two by the bandit's sharp blade.

It's just that it was no match for Alan's shovel.

"DIG!" Alan roared, aiming his shovel. With an eerie swooshing noise, he fired his Shovel Bolt. The shining blue beam of destructive light made direct contact with his opponent's weapon.

And just like that, the former Holy Knight's sword evaporated.

"Wha...?" The bandit leader looked down at his empty hands, lost for words.

"Boss, what're you playin' around for?" one of his minions asked.

The leader remained silent and unmoving. No surprise. Holy Knight training did not include circumstances in which their sword would be evaporated. This was beyond his comprehension.

"Boss...?" the other bandit said carefully. "What's going on?"

Another bandit snapped his fingers. "Wait, I know! The boss probably ditched his sword because he wants *us* to take care of this!"

"Oh, I get it!" the other said, jumping to a hasty conclusion. "Damn, you're smart! Let's get 'em!"

"Sir Miner!" The young lady with the golden locks and white dress finally spoke up. "Sir Miner, please... Please run!" Her long hair shook back and forth as she desperately pleaded with her would-be savior. "D-don't worry about me! You can't possibly win with just a shovel!"

For some reason, Alan couldn't help but smile at her words. He was genuinely happy. As far as he could tell, the young lady in question was just that—young, fifteen years old at most. And she was concerned for *his* well-being. Her own life was in danger, but here she was, worried about a stranger's safety. He admired the heck out of that.

I guess the surface folk ain't all bad in this day and age, after all.

Alan decided to go all out. He had to protect the young lady whose heart was as precious as any jewel; the young lady who would risk her life for a complete stranger.

"Engage power-up sequence." Alan said a bit melodramatically. For some reason, he felt like showing off a bit for the girl. Blue energy began to gather around his tool. It was the very concept of the shovel, turned into energy: the "Light of Digging." During the Jewel War, Alan had used this light to seal away the Emperor of Hell for all eternity.

"H-hey, let's scram! Everyone get the hell outta here! This guy ain't right!"

Only the bandit leader had noticed the Light of Digging. But it was too late.

The blue energy converged at the tip of the shovel. Alan gripped the handle tightly and released the safety lock. Power and targeting were a GO. Target: the bandits. Shovel recoil barrier: all green. Shoveling power charge: 120%.

"DIG!" he commanded.

KAAAAAA-BOOOOOOOOOMMM!!

The explosion of energy eradicated everything in its path. Alan called this particular technique the "Wave Motion Shovel Blast." The way he saw it, it was the essence of the shovel itself—a wave-like energy inherent in the process of digging and burying. At full power, it could harness the same amount of energy as the Big Bang, exploding outward in a bright blue wave beam. It was the ultimate shovel technique.

It was also, unsurprisingly, a bit difficult to aim.

The light beam passed directly over the bandits' heads, lancing past Alan's intended targets. Directly behind them was a mountain...emphasis on the *was*.

"Oh...shoot," Alan said. "Didn't mean to dig up the whole mountain..."

The entire natural structure had been annihilated by the Wave Motion Shovel Blast. He should have been more careful.

The bandits' jaws dropped to the ground, their mouths moving silently for a moment before delayed screams erupted from their throats.

"AAAAAAAAAAAHHHHHHHHHHH!!!"

"Huh...? Wait, what—aaaaaahhh!" Even the young lady in the white dress screamed in shock.

Everyone present looked at where the mountain once was, then back at Alan's shovel. Nobody could believe what they had just witnessed.

"Erm, m-my apologies." Alan caught the young lady just as she began to fall to the ground. "That was from the recoil of the Shovel Wave Motion Shovel Blast. I'm sorry; I went overboard."

"Shovel...Wave...Motion Gun?!" The girl raised her voice in shock.

"I really am sorry. I should have told you ahead of time to assume the anti-shovel defensive position."

"Wh-what?!" The young lady was on the verge of fainting.

This fateful encounter would go down in recorded history as the legendary first meeting between the miner and the princess.

PART 2

The Miner Has the Princess Do Whatever He Wants

AFTER THE BANDITS had been run off, Alan brought the girl back with him to his mountainside cottage.

"Thank you so very much!" The young lady with the beautiful golden locks—whose name, as it turned out, was Lithisia—bowed her head deeply to Alan. "I can't even begin to express how grateful I am for what you did today!"

"Don't worry about it. I just did what any miner would do."

A miner would save his companions when they were in danger. How could he not save a young girl in her time of need?

"Sir, you're a *miner*...? Not a knight?"

When Alan nodded his head in response, Lithisia's eyes glimmered with glee. "I had no idea that miners were so strong or could use magic!"

"Magic?"

"Yes! That incredible spell you unleashed! What kind of training did you have to undergo to use something like that?!" Lithisia asked.

"Hrm? You mean the Wave Motion Shovel Blast? I just focus my energy into my shovel, is all."

Lithisia was baffled by the miner's response. Then it dawned on her. "Focus your...? Ohhhh, I get it! It's a trade secret, isn't it?"

"And anyway, it's not magic, it's... Well, whatever." Apparently, the young lady had mistaken Alan for a miner who could use magic. He could spend his time correcting her, but it really wasn't worth the time or effort. It's not like she was hurting anyone with her incorrect deduction.

The real issue at hand was the girl's identity. As it so happened, she was the first in line for the throne of the grassland nation, Rostir—in other words, a real-and-true princess. Respected and beloved by citizens all over the country, who affectionately referred to her as "Her Royal Highness."

"I see..." Alan murmured after Lithisia explained this.

"Huh? You believe me?!"

"I see no reason why I shouldn't." She was beautiful, pure, and held herself in a royal manner. It was easy to believe she was a real princess.

"Thank you so much! I'm... I'm so moved!" Princess Lithisia began to tear up.

Alan decided to collect as much information from her as he could. This was his chance. "If possible, I'd like to ask you a few questions, Your Royal Highness."

"R-Royal Highness? No, no, please, just call me by my name." Lithisia waved her hands in a panic.

"That won't do. You're a princess and I'm just a miner."

"But you saved my life! Besides, you're older than me, are you not?"

"Yeah. I'm 1,011 years old this year."

"Huh?" Lithisia looked like she had been hit with a brick, but she soon recovered, looking a little embarrassed. "C-come now! I know I might be a naive little princess, but that's going too far!"

Alan blinked. *Wait, does she think I'm joking?*

"Even someone with demi-human blood could only live a hundred and fifty years at most. I've studied up on this!" Lithisia puffed out her chest with pride.

"Well, whatever..." Alan said. It wasn't his fault if the princess didn't believe him. He didn't blame her.

Instead, he began asking her a multitude of questions: Why was she traveling? Why didn't she have any guards with her? Finally, why had the bandits said she was worth a million gold coins?

Lithisia's face turned serious. "Rostir—my country— is in great danger."

She explained that a demon named Zeleburg was attempting to take over her nation. The demon was currently in the position of Prime Minister. When Lithisia's father, the king, died unexpectedly, Zeleburg stepped in to rule the country until Lithisia came of age. But the princess saw through the demon's scheme. She knew that it was the prime minister himself who had murdered her father, but she'd failed to convince others of his crimes.

"Zeleburg used a powerful charm to brainwash everyone in the royal palace," Lithisia went on. "No one would listen to me. They even tried to force me to marry him! If that were to happen, Zeleburg would become the king. I can't allow that. I refuse!" The princess held herself tightly, shaking her head with rage or fear or both.

"If this guy married you, he'd become the king?"

"That's right. I'm not just the princess; I'm the Rostir Royal Crown itself. Whoever I marry will inherit the legitimate right to the throne." She sighed. "That's why I can't choose a partner for myself. Whoever becomes my husband needs to be someone who could best serve as the king of Rostir. They must be skilled in battle, capable of seeing the truth, and possess a kindness above all others. They…"

Lithisia stopped abruptly.

"What's wrong?" Alan asked.

Lithisia's words then became unsteady as she looked Alan over. "Only someone...like that...could be the king..."

"Uh, Lithisia? Are you okay?"

"O-oh, no! I'm fine! It's nothing! Nothing at all!" For some reason, Princess Lithisia's cheeks went bright red as she shook her head briskly, as if trying to shake something off of her hair. "A-anyway, that's why I ran from the capital."

"Hrm. Do you have proof that this Zeleburg is a demon?"

"I do. He confessed when he killed my father."

"What an honest demon," Alan said wryly.

"I think...he knew that I was watching. He wanted me to hear that."

"Why?"

"He wanted me to feel true despair." Lithisia dropped her gaze. "He knows that, despite having seen the depths of his evil, I am powerless to stop him. Right now, I have a body double who remains in the capital, while I am treated as a fake who is sullying the good name of the princess, hence the bounty on my head. There is not a single soul in my country who believes me..."

"That's not true. I believe you."

Lithisia blinked rapidly. "Oh...Sir Miner..." She clasped her hands together and knelt down, almost as though she was offering him a prayer. "Thank you... Thank you so much..." Clearly moved by Alan's words, she offered her gratitude over and over.

Alan helped her to her feet, a little embarrassed by her display. "So, you ran away from the prime minister?"

"Yes, but I didn't just flee." Lithisia pulled a yellow jewel from the hem of her dress. Alan recognized it the moment he saw the intense magical light radiating from it.

"That's the Yellow Orb!" he exclaimed.

"It's one of my nation's treasures, passed down over the course of two thousand years. I'm surprised you know of it."

"Of course I do. I'm the one who dug that thing out of the ground. It was on the 4,328th layer, actually."

Lithisia tilted her head in confusion. "S-stop teasing me, Sir Miner!"

"No, seriously...."

"I know you're lying. After all, this was made hundreds of years ago!"

She was right—quite a bit of time had passed since Alan had dug it up. The orb was perhaps the most valuable thing he'd ever unearthed, and he still remembered it well.

On the 4,328th layer beneath the earth, Alan had discovered a glistening, rainbow-colored vein of gemstone. It had been guarded by a dragon with shining scales known as a Prismatic Wyrm. After a fierce battle to the death, Alan had dug the shining amber sphere out of the vein. His contact at the Mages' Guild had been ecstatic.

That gemstone had eventually been split by the Mages' Guild into the Orbs of Seven Colors, of which the Yellow Orb was one. It was said that all seven orbs, combined together, would create the ultimate magical tool.

And the Yellow Orb rested now in the hands of the Princess of Rostir. Alan couldn't help a small surge of pride to know that the jewel he'd dug up had become a national treasure. "Aren't there supposed to be six more of these?" he asked Lithisia.

"Wow! That's supposed to be top secret! You're something else, Sir Miner!"

Well, of course he'd know about that, being the one who'd mined it in the first place. But Alan wasn't about to waste time convincing her of that. "Well?" he pressed.

"Um, well...the rest of them were stolen," Lithisia said. She went on to explain that she'd directed the greatest mage in the country to use location magic to discover the whereabouts of the other six Orbs. However, none of them were in Rostir. They were scattered all over the continent. Beneath the sea, under the desert, above the clouds—all in places that were difficult, if not impossible, for humans to reach. Several recovery squads had been sent out, but none returned.

"It's said that if one gathers all seven Orbs together, they'll be granted a single wish. I have to get my hands on them, no matter what. When I do, I'll have Zeleburg and his minions exiled from the surface for all time," Lithisia explained as she hugged the Orb to her chest tightly.

"Hrm, so you're going to use your wish to save your kingdom..." It felt good to know that the jewels he'd discovered would be used for a noble cause.

"That's why I took the Yellow Orb and fled the palace. But those bandits showed up and...and then you saved me." Lithisia looked up at Alan. "Sir Miner, I...I have a request. I know I'm asking a lot of you, but it's because of who you are that I have to ask."

Alan knew where this was going and had no problem with it. "Understood. I'm on it."

"Could you help me search for the missing Orbs across the conti— Huh?" Lithisia stopped in her tracks and blinked multiple times. "S-Sir Miner, surely you jest! Please take this seriously!"

"I am," he replied. Locating the Orbs scattered across the land? How could there be anyone more perfect for the job than Alan himself? Besides, there was no way he'd be able to focus on his work knowing that the awesome jewels he'd unearthed had gone missing.

"Do you really understand? This will be a perilous journey."

"I'm a miner. Danger is my middle name."

"B-but I won't be able to pay you much…" Lithisia sadly lowered her shoulders. "Other than the Yellow Orb, all I currently have to my name is this dress."

"I figured."

"I'd be willing to do anything you ask of me after we reclaim my country."

"Anything?"

"Yes, anything. Is there something you desire, Sir Miner?"

Lithisia was the first in line for the throne of a massive nation. What could he ask of someone with so much power? After thinking it over for a bit, Alan realized there was only one thing he needed. "A successor."

Lithisia's expression froze upon hearing Alan's words. "…Huh?"

"For whatever reason, I'm perfectly healthy right now, but who knows when I might drop dead? After all, I'm an old man. I need a successor to take up my work after I'm gone." Alan felt this was a solid enough request. He would have Lithisia gather up prospective apprentices in her nation, and he'd interview them until he found someone worthy enough to succeed him as a jewel miner.

"Um, er, you mean...?" Oddly enough, Lithisia's cheeks were bright red. "B-by 'successor,' do you mean you want...a child?!"

"A child? Hrm...I suppose that's one direction we could go in." It wasn't an ideal solution, but it wasn't out of the question. Mining was a job that required one to hole themselves up in a mountain, and Alan didn't know how a child would adapt to that environment. He supposed he'd have to adopt a child, raise them in the mountain, and teach them everything he knew over time.

"I...I see... So I would have to... Sir Miner's child... Oh, dear..." Silence enveloped the room. Their eyes met, and Lithisia quickly averted her gaze. "Um, I'm sorry. I'm just awfully surprised..." The princess placed her hand over her ample breasts in an attempt to calm her racing heart.

"Hrm, I see..." Alan said. "Well, if you can't make it happen, I understand."

"No!" Lithisia shook her head fiercely. "Um, I-I told you I'd do anything, and I will! I-It's just...I had to prepare myself, is all!"

"Prepare yourself?"

"I-I'll do whatever it takes! I will! I'm no liar!" Lithisia took a deep breath, and her eyes hardened with determination. "I understand! I will make your child!"

Make my child? That certainly was an odd way of putting it, but Alan figured that royalty probably had their own way of doing things.

"I-I don't know much about making children, but I'll study up!"

"Take your time. You don't have to worry about this until we get back to your country."

Lithisia looked down at her own stomach and the space below the hem of her dress, then blushed beet-red. "G-good point. That would get in the way of our journey!"

"Yeah. You're right," Alan agreed. After all, scouring the land for potential apprentices would distract from their search for the Orbs of Seven Colors. "For now, I'll just think of other ways to get it done and practice."

"Practice?! Um, er, I..." Lithisia's ears reddened. "A-all right, I understand... I'll do my best," the princess responded as she fidgeted. "Practice...practice? Ohhhhhh..."

"Lithisia, your cheeks are flushed. Are you all right?"

"I-I'm totally fine! I have no problem with doing lewd things!"

"Wait, what?"

Alan and Lithisia had come to a mutual understanding...or, at least, they both *thought* they had.

"Ohhhhh...a child...a child...? What am I going to do...?" Lithisia brought both hands to her red-hot cheeks.

It would be quite some time before the princess discovered the error in her interpretation.

PART 3
The Miner Digs a Tunnel in Three Seconds

THE NEXT DAY, Alan and Lithisia began preparing for their journey. Alan didn't really need anything for himself, but he wasn't traveling alone this time. The princess had proudly volunteered to do all the packing for the tools in the cave, and spent some time in the storage shed gathering supplies.

"Sir Miner! Sir Miner! I've got everything packed up!" Lithisia excitedly proclaimed.

Alan looked over the contents of the bags. "Hrm... this is a little too much. You want to have at least twenty percent of the bag free."

"Why is that?"

"When traveling, it's extremely common to find yourself picking things up here and there. If your bags are full to begin with, you won't have much room for other items, and it'll only make the bag heavier for you to carry."

"I see! You're so wise, Sir Miner!" Not only was Lithisia an honest and innocent young lady, she was a ball of exuberant curiosity. Her eyes bounced all over the storage shed. "Wow...so miners use all of these tools? There must be hundreds here!"

"Yeah, I suppose. But I just stick with my handy shovel."

A few hundred years ago, Alan had used all manner of pickaxes and drills. Nowadays, he could pretty much get by with just his shovel. This was fortunate, considering how difficult it was to haul all of the other equipment into the deepest depths.

"I see... So you're saying the shovel is the most important tool of all?" Lithisia stared at one of the shovels standing against the wall, an aura of wonder emanating from her gaze. "Wow...that's amazing! It's so cool!"

"Lithisia, would you like to bring one with you?"

"Are...are you serious?! Oh please, may I?"

Alan began rummaging through one of his boxes. It was there that he located a red shovel about eight inches long, made for children rather than serious mining work.

"Oh wow, it's so small and red. It's adorable! Can I really have this?!"

Alan nodded.

Lithisia took the shovel from him, holding it in both hands like it was the most valuable treasure on the planet. "I...I'm going to make this one of the royal family's treasures! It will be sacred to my bloodline forever!"

"Er...you're kidding, right? That's just a children's shovel."

Lithisia ignored him. "Hee hee, my own shovel! One that Sir Miner used!"

Why was she so happy? Well, whatever her reasons, Alan was nonetheless pleased that she placed so much value on her new shovel. "By the way, Lithisia. It's about time we talked about our destination."

"Huh? Oh, of course! My apologies!" Slightly flustered, the princess made her way toward the table. "Let me show you on the map. Our first destination is in the west: the Ancient Castle of Riften."

They were currently located in the southwestern region of the continent, the edge of Rostir. There were no human nations further west. There used to be one about three hundred years ago, but it was annihilated in the great War of Genocide between the humans and the monsters. In the end, humanity was victorious, but at great cost. Riften had been annihilated.

According to Lithisia, the Ancient Castle of Riften was where the next Orb resided.

"In order to get there, we have to travel along the coast," Lithisia explained in a formal, imperious tone. "The prime minister's lackies will be after us, so it'll be dangerous, but there are no other roads to Riften. I'm prepared to travel in spite of the danger."

Alan cast his gaze upon the map. He thought for a moment before speaking. "If there are no other roads, why don't we make one?" He pointed at the map. "It would be faster to travel in a straight line to Riften. The Rostir Mountain Range is in the way, but all we'd have to do is cut a road through it."

"Er, what?" Lithisia was taken aback for a moment, but then began to laugh. "Hee hee. Oh, Sir Miner. Making a road is no easy task!"

"Really?"

"But of course! It's incredibly difficult. It takes decades for a country to construct a single road."

"Even harder to make than tunnels?"

"Tunnels are even more difficult to make! It costs lots of money to dig a road underground." Lithisia proudly puffed out her chest, happy to show off her education.

"Is that so? I had no idea…"

"I'm so honored I could teach you something, Sir Miner!" She giggled, playing with her hair. Princess Lithisia had a childish side to her, now and then.

"Well, then," Alan said. "I guess that means it's time for me to teach you something. As long as you have a shovel, you can build a road."

Lithisia froze in place. "Huh? Um, what do you mean?"

"Watch." Alan pointed the tip of his shovel at a point on the wall. The wall was made of solid stone, but as far as the miner was concerned, that stone was as soft as the skin of a young maiden. "DIG!" he shouted.

The wall flared up in a blinding white light. "Ahh!" Lithisia cried, shielding her face. The light faded a few seconds later, and the princess slowly opened her eyes. In the place where the wall once stood was a large tunnel about six feet in diameter. Lithisia stared at it, mouth agape.

"That tunnel's about a mile long," Alan estimated. "If I do this ten more times, we'll be past the mountain."

"Um, e-excuse me, Sir Miner. What...what did you just do?"

"I dug a tunnel with my shovel."

"Wh-what? Huh?" Lithisia could hardly believe her ears. "You...dug a tunnel? Just like that? One that big?"

"Yeah."

"It didn't look like you even moved!"

"Yeah. I just dug so fast that you couldn't see it."

Alan went on to explain that the more one practiced digging with a shovel, the faster one got. At first, it took

Alan ten minutes to dig three feet. After practicing for a year, he brought that time down to five minutes. Ten years later and he had it down to three minutes. A century later, it only took him a minute. He kept getting faster. Ten seconds, then one.

The one-second mark was where he realized he wouldn't be able to dig any faster. The physics of the world just didn't operate like that, so Alan changed his way of thinking. He decided to just ignore physics and logic altogether.

It took him a hundred years to break past the one-second wall, but after practicing endlessly, he managed to cut the process of digging three feet down to microseconds.

"Huh?" Lithisia's eyes widened in confusion.

"I focus my energy into the shovel and ignore the physics of our world."

"Excuse me, but I'm not sure I follow."

"I didn't either, at first. But all it takes is some tinkering."

"Tinkering?" she repeated.

"That being said, it isn't easy. It requires lots of practice."

"Practice? Wh-what...?" Tears began to form in Lithisia's eyes. "That's your shovel's true power?" The princess clutched her red shovel tightly as she trembled. "Does that mean the beam which destroyed the mountain the other day wasn't some kind of grand magic, but the power of your shovel?!" As soon as Alan nodded, Lithisia broke down into sobs. "I'm so sorry! I can't believe how ignorant I am..."

"Er, it's no big deal. Don't cry."

"How could I not cry?! What have I done?"

Lithisia continued to sob as Alan gently rubbed her back. A split-second later, her head jerked up and she was all smiles again, just like that.

"I've made my decision!" she declared. "When I take back my country, all knights will be required to wield shovels!"

"Um, what?" Alan was totally lost. What was the princess going on about? "What about their swords?"

Lithisia laughed. "Swords? Magic? What good are they compared to the mightiest weapon of all, the shovel?"

"Um..."

"How have we overlooked its powers this whole time? The shovel will revolutionize war as we know it!"

"Lithisia, hold your horses." The young princess was so excited that she wasn't paying attention to him. "The reason the shovel works as my weapon is because I'm a miner. Knights are supposed to use swords."

"But Sir Miner, it's impossible to pull off your shovel techniques with a sword."

"Not necessarily," Alan said. Maybe if the knights practiced focusing their energies into the sword, that might actually work. He figured if the shovel could overcome the natural laws of the world, the sword should be able to as well.

Lithisia ignored him, determined to honor the shovel. "We should write a song for the shovel!" she said. "Shovel time, shovel time~"

"Lithisia..."

"You know what? I should rename the country! Instead of Rostir, we could be Shovelir!"

"*Lithisia.*"

"In that case, I can change my name to Shovisia! The sky's the shovelimit!" Lithisia giggled to herself as she rubbed her red shovel against her face, as if she were nuzzling a kitten.

Although the princess seemed to be having fun, Alan couldn't help but sigh. "Royalty sure are strange folk," he muttered.

And so Lithisia became a firm believer in the shovel. This was also the moment in which the future of all Rostir knights was set in stone. Sad, sad, stone.

"I can't believe I did that right in front of you...ugh..."

"I was surprised, sure, but don't worry about it."

With Lithisia having finally regained her composure, the pair made their way down the path. She wore a rucksack on her back, with her shovel at her waist. These mining-girl accessories didn't quite match her princessy dress, but she looked happy enough to start skipping.

"Lithisia, if you're that excited about the shovel, then I know I can count on you to find me a successor."

"Eh...? Ah!" said the princess as she froze. Her cheeks immediately warmed up, turning a soft pink. It was as if she'd just gotten out of the bath. "O-of course! Um, I-I'm honored."

"Honored? By what?"

"I...I can't possibly say it out loud! It's too embarrassing!"

Why was she so flustered? Alan didn't quite understand. Nonetheless, the pair continued to trudge forward. Lithisia went quiet for a bit before finally speaking again.

"Sir Miner, I have another request." She gripped her little red shovel in both hands, her tone growing serious. "Please, teach me how to use a shovel!"

"Heeyah!"

Lithisia used both hands to stick her red shovel into the dirt wall.

"Nicely done. Your form is excellent."

"Yay! Thank you so much!" Lithisia replied excitedly. "So this is how it feels to wield a shovel! Just holding it in my hands makes me feel like the power of a hero is flowing through my veins!"

Obviously, shovels didn't have that sort of inherent power. What Lithisia was wielding was just an ordinary old shovel. But the princess would hear nothing of the sort. In fact, she was on the verge of breaking out into a dance as she sang her shovel song.

Seriously, what is with that song? Alan wondered.

Maybe he should reconsider the whole "teaching her how to shovel" thing. Using a shovel required immense physical strength and fortitude. It wasn't the sort of tool of a member of royalty—never mind a gentle princess— should be using. Or at least that was what Alan attempted to explain to his companion.

"What are you saying, Sir Miner?!" Lithisia said in a furious rebuttal. "Wielding a shovel is a sacred duty, the job of every person of royalty!"

"I highly doubt that."

"No, it's true! I'll be including it as one of the requirements of the royal family going forward!" Alan thought the royal family was in for some rough times in the near future. "P-plus, as a mother, I need to make sure I learn how to wield a shovel properly."

"What do you mean, 'as a mother'?"

"Well, I am going to be making a child, after all..." Lithisia shyly hid her lips behind her shovel. "So I want to learn all about your, um...work, Sir Miner."

"Well, I suppose I don't mind."

"Thank you so much! I-I'll make sure to make a healthy child!" replied Lithisia as she bowed her head over and over.

"By the way, Lithisia," Alan said. "You should probably stop saying you're going to 'make a child'."

"Huh?"

"Depending on who's listening in, it could give folks the wrong idea."

Even if that was the official way royalty referred to the act, should a commoner hear a phrase like that, they'd most certainly think the princess was referring to "a couple making love." Folks might make the mistake of thinking that a beautiful princess like her was romantically involved with a dirty miner.

Although Alan didn't know it, this was exactly what the princess intended.

"Oh, um...so you want this to be a secret between the two of us?"

"Not quite. I just think you should adjust your wording is all."

"O-oh, okay. So it's like a secret lovey-dovey code between us!"

Alan decided not to comment. He had already long since decided that this princess was a bit funny in the head.

After thinking to herself for a moment, Lithisia seemed to have an epiphany. "Then from now on, instead of saying 'I'll make a child'..." She then held her red shovel to her chest, her cheeks and ears turning bright red. "I'll refer to it as 'shoveling.'"

A cold gust of wind blew through the tunnel.

"I-Is that all right? Since it's something I'll be doing together with you, Sir Miner, I thought 'shoveling' might be appropriate."

Alan went silent. Why would looking for a successor need to be coded as "shoveling"?

But if I say no here...

Lithisia's eyes were shimmering. She wore the expression of a young girl begging for a new toy. It was the same look she had when she'd asked for a shovel. If Alan were to say no here, she'd probably break down into tears. "I'm so so so sorry, I shouldn't have shoveled!" she'd say. He could see it clear as day.

"Well, fine."

"Thank you so much!" She bowed so deeply that Alan thought she might topple over. "Th-then in that case..." She pressed her shovel firmly to her chest and smiled. "I promise to 'shovel' together with you, Sir Miner."

"Uh, sure." Much to Alan's surprise, the look the princess was giving him made his heart flutter. *No, no. What am I thinking?* Alan activated his self-control, trying to be strong as adamantine.

And so the misunderstanding continued.

THE INVINCIBLE
SHOVEL

Lithisia and Her Naked Shovel

IT WAS SEVEN IN THE EVENING, and Lithisia was seated on her knees inside the tent. Her mind raced, knowing she was facing her first night together with her miner.

Aaaaaahhh, what do I do?! I-I'm so nervous!

Her heart was racing a mile a minute. Why? Once the miner returned from hunting, they would practice "shoveling" on their very first night together.

If one were to put it into numbers, Lithisia was 100% excited and 300% losing her mind. She was so panicked that she didn't consider the mathematical impossibility of it. After all, she was just a naive princess. Of course, she understood the general process of how to make a child. One became naked, and then, well, lewd things transpired.

But she was shaken up. Not over doing lewd things, but whether or not she would be able to satisfy the miner. Lithisia was considered the most beautiful young woman in Rostir, but she wondered if her looks meant anything to the great and noble miner, Alan. At the end of the day, she was beautiful by *human* standards. What if the dwarven-blooded miner had different standards altogether? What if he preferred women with a shovel-like face? What would she do?

She glanced down at the shovel in her hands. It was then that an entirely foolish idea took root in Lithisia's mind.

"Perfect!" she squealed.

Meanwhile, Alan was out hunting with his trusty shovel. He had already finished off a wild boar by digging a hole with his tool. He butchered the meat with the blade of the shovel, then cooked it using Shovel Fire. After preserving the meat in his Shovel Fridge, he returned to where the princess was waiting for him. He had once heard that those in the palace ate wild boar meat, so he was hopeful that Lithisia would be pleased. It was her first time camping, after all, and he thought it'd be nice if he could help her relax.

Lithisia was raised as a princess. She was a delicate flower. Although Alan struggled at times to understand her words and actions, he knew that she must be nervous about going on a journey like this.

Determined to be her protector, Alan returned to the tent only to find Lithisia looking for all the world like her body was covered with nothing but a shovel.

"What the—?"

The line from Lithisia's ample breasts to her hips was silky smooth, shaped vaguely like the contours of a gardening shovel. Her attractive thighs, much like her breasts, looked far softer than any soil that Alan could ever dig up.

WHOA, WHOA, WHOA! Alan quickly shook his head in an attempt to free his mind from all the shoveling metaphors he was coming up with to describe the vision before him. *Stay calm, stay calm*, he quietly told himself over and over again before looking back at Lithisia.

Upon closer inspection, she was not in fact fully naked. She was at least wearing panties, but that was it. Most of her bosom was bare for all to see, and her smooth thighs were visible. The garter belt she wore made them stand out even more. This glimpse at her nearly nude body was in fact far more suggestive than if she simply wore nothing at all.

In Lithisia's hands was a single shovel. "Um, um, um, er, um, um..." The princess herself was an embarrassed mess. She squirmed uncomfortably, her ears cherry red. Her adorable motions caused her white panties to ride up a little.

With each move she made, her unconscious attack on Alan's self-control continued. She then looked up at him. "W-welcome home, Sir Miner...! W-would you like dinner, a bath, or perhaps..." Lithisia squeezed her thighs together and leaned forward, emphasizing the shape of her breasts. "...you'd like to 'shovel' with me?"

It was as though time itself had frozen. Alan finally spoke. "...Lithisia."

"Yes?!"

"I think you've got this shoveling thing all wrong."

Lithisia's thoughts crashed down to the ground with a *thud*.

⊳━━━━━━━►

It took several minutes before Lithisia was able to speak properly again. "W-will you ever be able to forgive me?" she begged.

"What's there to forgive? You haven't done anything wrong."

"B-but I tried to do the Naked Shovel and failed..."
Lithisia cried.

She wasn't wrong. It was pretty stupid. In all of Alan's
thousand-plus years of life, he'd never seen something so
misguided.

"I've sullied the good name of the shovel. The only way
I can make amends is by ending my life...!" She took the
tip of her red shovel and held it up to her throat. Alan
panicked and took the tool from her.

"Don't do that! It's not a capital offense!"

"I'm first in line for the throne. When I take my country back, I can make it one!"

"Don't." The last thing Rostir needed was a wave of
executions. "Look, it's really not a big deal. Hell, I've mis-
used the shovel before."

"What?!" Lithisia could hardly believe her ears.

"My father would scold me all the time. 'You couldn't
even shovel sand with the limp way you hold that thing'.
So I practiced as much as I could. I watched the way my
father worked, memorized how to hold a shovel properly, how to put power into one. I practiced for ages. It
was only recently that I figured out how to fire the Wave
Motion Shovel Blast."

"Erm, the Wave Motion Shovel Blast...?"

Lithisia clearly had something on her mind, but Alan

barreled along. "Correct. So don't worry about it. One day you'll get used to it like I did."

Lithisia held her mouth slightly ajar in surprise. She looked relatively satisfied by his explanation.

"And uh, put on some clothes."

"Huh...? Ahh!!" The young princess finally remembered the state she was in. "I-I'm so sorry! I'm sure it must pain you to have to look at a body like mine..." Lithisia quickly pulled her cape over her body and lowered her eyes to the floor.

"No, not at all. You're, um..."

"What?"

Alan was unsure whether he should continue. Was it really all right to say something like this to a fifteen-year-old young lady? At the same time, it would be rude *not* to say anything, so he steeled his resolve. As his mind recalled the sight of Lithisia clad in only panties and a shovel...

"...quite attractive," he finished with an embarrassed cough.

"Oh...!"

"Your skin is soft and white, and your hair is transparent, like an angel's. I honestly couldn't believe my eyes. So, um, just be careful from now on, okay?" If Alan's self-restraint were weaker, he would've been done in by the sight of her nearly naked body.

"I-I see...um, like an a-angel...? Aaah..." Lithisia's heart was pierced in that moment not by Cupid's arrows, but something more like Cupid's shovel.

"All right, you can have this back now."

Alan gave her back the red shovel. He didn't simply hand it to her, but instead, made sure her gentle hands were holding it the proper way. He had all ten of her fingers grip the handle, and confirmed that she would never have the edge of the shovel facing towards her.

Time and time again their hands met, Alan's rough and Lithisia's soft. "Sir Miner, your hands are so rugged..."

"Lithisia, this is how you're supposed to hold a shovel. Got it memorized?"

After some time, the golden-haired princess looked up at Alan and continued to stare into his eyes. Finally, her cheeks turned bright red and she averted her gaze. "Y-yes..." Lithisia pressed the palm of her hand to her bountiful breasts. She could still feel Alan's warmth on her skin. "I'll never forget the way this feels...ever."

Alan was relieved that she understood. Her reaction was a bit odd, but he figured that was because she was a naive princess. "Glad to hear it. How about we eat?" Alan rose to his feet and began to prepare the wild boar.

He was already out of earshot when Lithisia spoke again.

"Sir Miner, I've got it memorized. I finally understand, at last." The tears wouldn't stop falling from her eyes. "A shovel is something that envelops and forgives all..." Lithisia gripped her red shovel in front of her chest. "A shovel is the world itself... Yes, I've got it memorized!"

Alan had yet to realize that Lithisia was already too far gone to be dissuaded from her shovel worship.

PART 4
The Miner Saves Catria

AFTER EXITING THE TUNNEL, the pair traveled across a field of green for a time before Lithisia alerted Alan of their location. "Sir Miner, we'll be arriving in one of the border towns momentarily."

Alan took another look at Lithisia. Despite the amount of time she spent in the tunnel, her white dress was as radiant as ever. It was as if it had a kind of dirt-dispelling magic applied to it. Her beautiful golden locks, refined mannerisms, and perfect figure announced to anyone looking that she was royalty. She'd stick out like a sore thumb. They would have to get her some kind of disguise.

"There's a military fortress there, yeah?" Alan said. "We'll have to make sure you don't get spotted."

"Um, Sir Miner? Wh-when you keep staring at me like that, I..." Lithisia squirmed and covered her breasts with her arms.

"My apologies."

"No, no! It's fine! I was just surprised is all! You can look as much as you want!" Lithisia quickly added. "Since we'll be 'shoveling' together in the future, I-I'd rather have you look!"

What did shoveling and staring at her have to do with one another? Alan had questions, but opted to put them aside. The key to dealing with the princess was to not think too deeply about anything she said. "Anyway, you said there's a fortress in the town we're coming up on, yeah? What sort of numbers are we talking?"

"Um, there are a hundred and eight soldiers in the border squad of the Knights of Rostir."

"Well, aren't you a font of knowledge?"

"W-well, I *am* royalty." Lithisia looked happy to receive the compliment. She scratched at her cheek, slightly embarrassed. "B-because I'm a princess, I have a friend in the Knights of Rostir. She's a very talented knight with a bright future ahead of her. She even vowed to dedicate her life to me!"

"Huh. Sounds like a keeper."

"She is! If you ignore her two problems, she's the perfect knight."

"Problems?"

"She's...kind of lacking in ability."

"Er, isn't that usually fatal when it comes to being a knight?"

"Actually, it pales in comparison to the second problem she has."

"Which is?"

"She wields a sword, not a shovel."

Alan considered saying something, but opted to keep his mouth shut.

"But..." Lithisia visibly grew a bit sullen. "I'm most certain that she'll see me as an enemy now."

The Lithisia in the palace was fake, and the one here was real, but Alan was the only person who believed that. "Hrm...then for now, we should be careful not to draw the attention of these knights."

"Understood." Lithisia nodded her head.

Just then, the high-pitched sound of metal colliding with metal rang out.

Alan narrowed his eyes. "Looks like someone's fighting."

As the sun began to set on the grasslands, a fierce battle was taking place. It was still far in the distance, but miners had excellent vision—especially Alan. In fact, he could see the radiant shine of a jewel from over six miles away. This was a talent expected of all jewel miners.

It was with this exceptionally sharp sight that Alan made out three men and one woman in the distance. They all wore the same shining white armor.

"Knights. A red-haired female knight is being attacked by the others."

"Huh...? Red hair? Could that be Catria?!"

"Your friend?"

"Yes! The very same knight I was telling you about earlier! Ah, Catria!"

Alan nodded in response and drew his shovel.

"Sir Miner, we must run! We have to save her!"

"There's no need to run."

"Huh? What do you mean?"

Instead of explaining, Alan rested his shovel on his shoulder and targeted the knights in the distance.

Alan's shovel was the strongest close-range weapon imaginable. Alan had come to that conclusion when he conquered the Shrine of the Ancient Titan on Layer #555 of the mountain. The king of all titans wielded a giant axe, but the miner was able to split it in two with one slash of his shovel. It was then that he realized just how powerful his shovel was.

His thoughts on the matter were different now. Not only was the shovel an amazing close-range weapon...

"No worries. I can reach them from here."

The shovel was also the most powerful *long*-range weapon in the world.

Catria was a knight because she'd had no other choice but to become one.

She had two older sisters, both of whom were tremendously beautiful. But her family, House Eugenohl, boasted a generations-old lineage of proud knights, and they couldn't keep up that tradition with only daughters. Her father had prayed every day, rain or shine, to the Earth Goddess for a boy.

His prayers were answered with a firm "no" when Catria was born. When the young girl heard this tale from her nanny, she wept. She finally understood why her father looked upon her with such sad eyes. She sobbed, and sobbed, and when she had finally grown tired of the tears, Catria gripped a sword in her hands. "I *will* become a knight," she vowed. A knight her father could be proud of: a Holy Knight, the highest-ranking knight of them all.

Ten years passed. Catria had practiced until her arms were swollen and her feet were blistered beyond belief, and somehow, she'd managed to get a shot at the entrance exam for the King's Knights. In a one-on-one duel with a knight's apprentice, she came out victorious. She was beyond excited. Maybe now her father would be proud of her!

But mere minutes later, Catria overheard something in the crowd she shouldn't have, and her smile shattered.

"It must be so frustrating to lose on purpose. Just what is that Eugenohl girl thinking?"

Catria fled, her heart shattered once again upon overhearing those words. Of course the knights would lose on purpose to someone who outranked them. She wept and wept, knowing she would never truly be a knight on her own merits.

But as fate would have it, Princess Lithisia had been observing the Knights of Rostir on that day.

"I want her as my bodyguard." Lithisia said upon seeing Catria. She had been inspecting the fortress when she made that declaration. Quite frankly, Catria had no idea why she'd been picked. If the princess simply wanted a woman by her side, there were other, better options. At first, she thought that maybe she was chosen because she was of House Eugenohl, but Princess Lithisia didn't know what she looked like, and couldn't have picked her out on sight. So, was it her ability as a knight? That couldn't be it, either. She was the weakest of the knights.

Eventually, Catria asked Lithisia that very question.

"It's because your eyes shone the most out of anyone's!" Lithisia had told her. Catria didn't know what to say to that. Her eyes had been glistening because she'd been crying.

"By the way, Catria," the princess went on, dramatically, "it seems to me like you're not very good at swordplay. But don't worry! One day, you'll be the greatest Holy Knight on the continent. "Why? Because I said so, and what the princess says, goes! That's a fact!"

Catria was in shock, but Lithisia simply smiled. "Hee hee. Got it, Catria? Become an amazing Holy Knight and protect me, okay?"

Lithisia winked at her.

To Catria, she looked like a brilliant beam of light. This princess had what she didn't, and yet she expected great things from her.

It was on that day that Catria swore absolute fealty to Princess Lithisia.

At present, the sun was setting over the grasslands as Catria found herself facing off against three knights.

"I WON'T LOSE!" she roared, even knowing her chances were slim. Those knights had been sent to retrieve a fugitive...namely, her.

When the king was assassinated, Catria just happened to be in the capital, taking her sick father's place at the funeral. Concerned that she couldn't find Lithisia, she made her way to the princess' room. It was there that she overheard something she shouldn't have: a conversation between Prime Minister Zeleburg and Lithisia's body double. She'd gasped, and that had given her away.

"Who's there?!" Zeleburg had shouted.

Catria had fled the palace, becoming a fugitive in the process. She could no longer return to the knights. She could no longer go anywhere. She had to find the princess.

"Aaaaaaah!" she shouted as she traded blows with the knights. Catria stood no chance of victory against even one of them, but nonetheless, she couldn't afford to fall here. She was the only one who could save her beloved princess, or so she believed. That thought kept her standing, desperately swinging her sword.

"You'll be the greatest Holy Knight on the continent."

Lithisia's words echoed in her head. For the sake of her beloved, radiant princess, Catria could not afford to lose.

"Come on!" Catria taunted. She thrust her sword forward with every ounce of power she had. *Reach. Reach. REACH!!!*

"As if!" laughed one of the knights.

"Wha—?!"

Clank! Catria's sword was sent flying by one of the knights.

"You don't even have the basics down, rookie." The knight swept her legs out from under her, causing her to tumble to the ground. He pointed his sword at her. "Catria Eugenohl, for the sin of desertion, you will be executed here and now."

Her sword was long gone. But that just meant she'd have to fight with her two hands. The moment she attempted to move, however, the knight's white blade quickly moved to her neck. There was nothing she could do. It was over.

"If you have any last words, I'll relay them to Lord Eugenohl."

She began to sob in despair. "I... I...."

Why am I so weak? she cursed herself.

In order to live up to her father's and Lithisia's expectations, she'd thrown herself into her training. That sword thrust she attempted mere moments ago was the product of months of training, and yet, she was told she didn't have the basics down.

It was as if her very heart had been cut from her chest.

"What the princess says, goes! That's a fact!"

Catria recalled Princess Lithisia's words, but they only made the pain worse, causing more tears to roll down her cheeks. She had to save the woman who gave her a reason to live, but she couldn't. After all the hard work she put in, why was her goal so unattainable?

"Catria... As a knight and as a person..." the knight above her intoned, plunging her into the depths of despair. "You're nothing but a weakling."

She closed her eyes. The sword came swinging down.

KA-CHOOOOOOOOOM!

The knight was sent flying high into the air. His screams echoed throughout the grasslands.

Catria jerked her head up in surprise. "...Huh?"

KA-CHOOOOOOOOOM!

The slightly goofy roar rang out a second time, but despite the way it sounded, its power was tremendous. The knight had been hurled almost a thousand feet into the sky. He was in the air for several seconds before he came crashing down in front of Catria.

BA-BOOM!

The dent in the earth where the knight had once stood was the same shape as the head of a shovel.

Boom! Kerplow! Bam! One after the other, the rest of the knights were sent flying.

"What the heck...?" was all Catria could manage.

"Reloading."

"Yaaay, hooray! You're amazing, Sir Miner!"

Alan aimed at the knights from the top of the hill and pulled the "Shovtrigger," which was what he called the shovel's handle.

Ka-choom! A roughly triangular mass of blue, glimmering energy fired out of the end of the shovel. This was Alan's trusty "Shovel Launcher." By using the power contained within the shovel, he could convert earth into energy bullets. While this sounded impossible to anyone else, it made perfect sense to Alan. Since he could fire these energy bullets with pinpoint accuracy, it was a skill entirely suited to saving friends in need during combat.

Reloading the Shovel Launcher simply required scooping up some more dirt from the ground. "All right," Alan said. "Reloading complete."

The Shovel Launcher was handy in that it could fire off continuous shots. Much better suited for long term combat than the Wave Motion Shovel Blast.

"Beginning second wave. Fire!"

Ka-choom, ka-choom! With each shot, the knights in the distance went flying.

"Sir Miner, why are the knights flying through the air?!"

"A shovel taps into the power of the earth itself, and said knights are standing upon the earth, so it flings them upward," he explained.

"I'm not sure I follow, but either way, that's shovel-tastic!"

"Last shovel." Alan fired off the last shot from his Shovel Launcher.

"D-dat wash amwazing! I'm shovely moved!"

"Calm down, Lithisia. You're talking all weird."

"Sho what?!" Princess Lithisia was vibrating with excitement, her eyes shining. Her imagination was clearly starting to go in some weird directions.

Alan sighed. "Well, whatever. Let's save this Catria of yours."

"Oh, yes! That's right! Catria!" Lithisia waved her hands over her head as she descended the hill. Alan followed soon after, passing her quickly and arriving at the young knight's location a little before the princess.

Catria sat on the ground in silence, her fiery red hair tied into a ponytail. She looked to be a bit older than Lithisia, and while she was wearing white armor, her thighs were bare beneath her short skirt. She sat with her hands at her sides, like her legs had given out. She was so defenseless that Alan actually felt bad for her.

The miner extended a helping hand to the knight. "Sorry to keep you waiting," he said. He gave her a once-over. "Hmm...you're hurt."

Crouching down, Alan began to wrap a bandage around Catria's thigh.

"Wh-who are you...?" Catria asked shakily.

"The wound seems shallow. Not bad, considering you were facing off against three opponents."

"Huh?" He had been watching her? He saw her failure? Tears began to form in her eyes.

"Why are you crying? Does it hurt?"

"N-no, that's not it... I'm not crying...!"

It was clear as day that she was crying. She must've taken her earlier loss hard. After thinking for a moment, Alan spoke. "You're Catria, yes? I watched your battle, and quite frankly, you have a long way to go."

"I—"

"That was one helluva thrust. You have talent. What a waste."

"...Huh?" Alan's words were unexpected. "Wh-what did you just say?" *Me? Talent?* she thought. *And who is this guy, anyway?*

"Catria! Catria! Are you all right?!"

The knight's expression changed the moment she saw the girl approaching them. She was beautiful and innocent, clad in a blindingly white dress. "What?! P-Princess Lithisia?!"

"That's me!" giggled the princess as she took Catria's hands in her own. "It's been too long, Catria. I'm glad you're safe."

"Your Royal Highness... I... I'm so happy you're all right!"

"I thought I'd never see you again," Lithisia told her with a smile. "I'm shovely happy!"

A gust of wind blew through the grasslands. Catria thought for a moment that she'd misheard the princess. But Lithisia instead smiled as brightly as the sun and repeated herself.

"I'm *shovely* happy!" The second time she said it, she emphasized the "shovely." There was no mistaking it.

"Your Royal Highness, could you...give me a second?"

"I'd be shovely pleased to wait!"

What is she saying? What's wrong with my princess?! Catria thought. "Um, wh-what exactly do you mean by 'shovely happy'?"

"In our great nation, 'shovely' means 'extremely'! It's a new rule I just made!"

Catria was completely and utterly lost. "Um...I...huh?!"

"Lithisia, stop," Alan chided her. "Even I'm getting confused. 'Shovely' isn't a word."

"Now, now. Don't be humble. The shovel is great and wise! It is the evolution of communication itself!"

"It really isn't."

This back-and-forth went on for a bit until Catria grew impatient and interrupted. "Wait, hold your horses! Who exactly are you? Why are you with Princess Lithisia?"

"I'm Alan, and I'm a miner. While the princess goes on her journey, I'm serving as her bodyguard."

"A miner...? Why would a miner be tasked with guarding the princess? What have you done to her?" Catria cast her gaze upon the shovel that hung casually from Alan's right hand. "And what's with that shovel?"

"Catria, please calm down," Lithisia said. "I simply promised to 'shovel' with him; that's all."

The knight turned blue in the face. "Your Royal Highness, please! Pull yourself together! You're not making sense!"

"I'm feeling shovely fine!" She shovely was not.

Catria desperately tried to bring Lithisia back to reality.

"Shovels are merely tools for digging up dirt! Please try to remember!"

"That's not true, Catria. Shovels are divine."

"Like God?!"

"Actually, they're more than divine."

"Above that?!" What was she *talking* about?

"Indeed. Just the other night, Sir Miner taught me the true greatness of the shovel!"

"I don't ever recall that happening," Alan added, but he was totally ignored. Lithisia was clearly on some kind of shovel high.

Catria turned her fury on the miner. "Grrr...you bastard! How dare you brainwash the princess?!"

"What? I didn't brainwash her!"

Sadly, Catria didn't appear to be in a listening mood. Her eyes burned with anger. "That's it! Prepare yourself!"

She swung her blade, but she was slower than a regular knight. To the greatest miner on the planet, she was slower than a slug crawling its way along a tunnel. Alan dodged Catria's attack and tapped his shovel against her neck.

"Gah!" The knight collapsed to the floor, unconscious.

"Catria?!" Lithisia cried.

"She'll be fine," Alan reassured her. "I just hit one of her pressure points. If anything, she'll feel great when she wakes up."

"Oh, okay! Thank goodness! Shovels are shovmazing."

"Princess, *please* stop making up new words. Just say 'so amazing' like normal people." Alan sighed. How was he going to explain this to Catria when she woke up?

Lithisia ignored him and knelt to stroke her friend's hair. "Get a good shovrest, Catria."

Alan sighed once more as he set his gaze upon Lithisia watching over Catria like some sort of saint. Maybe he was just screwed.

"**H**EY! Let me out of here this instant!"

Catria's hair was as disheveled as the rest of her when she awoke. She'd found herself in a hole that could've been made by an antlion. Alan had felt bad about tying her up with rope, so instead he made a simple jail cell for her with his shovel. It was about three feet in diameter. Its walls had been hardened using alkaline excretions from the shovel, so it was completely smooth and impossible for anyone but Alan to climb.

"My apologies, Sir Miner. Catria is a little bit confused," Lithisia explained while sitting on her knees and watching her friend.

"Yeah, she is. Mostly because of you."

"I completely understand. She must be shocked that I'm safe."

"Actually, I'd say it's more your words and actions that've shocked her."

But of course, Lithisia wasn't actually listening. The princess had a tendency to ignore his comments. "I'll take responsibility and explain everything to her."

"Please don't. I get the feeling that letting you take charge would be a very bad idea."

"But I'm Catria's master. I think I'm shovely perfect for the job."

"Nope. Definitely shovely not. I'll handle this."

"Really? That's too bad, but I suppose I'll leave the matter in your hands."

I can't believe that worked, Alan thought. Even as someone used to working with a shovel, the princess' eccentricity was enough to throw him for a loop. He could totally relate to Catria's confusion.

A while later, Alan climbed into the hole and sat next to Catria. He tried to explain the situation to her, but the knight was having none of it.

"Impossible! Like hell I believe any of that!" Catria shouted with rage. "You dug a tunnel six miles long with your shovel? You defeated those knights earlier with your

Shovel Rifle? You might think you can fool the princess, but you'll never fool a knight like me! You're nothing but a fraud!"

Just as Alan was struggling to determine his next move, Lithisia spoke up. "Sir Miner! Why don't you scoop up her heart with your shovel?"

"What are you talking about...?" Alan asked. Lithisia's communicative abilities were rapidly falling apart.

"Grr...if only I had my sword. I'd cut you down!" Catria threatened as she bravely stared down the miner.

"Do you really think you can defeat me?"

"Of course! A sword would never lose to a shovel!"

Lithisia excitedly chimed in. "Sir Miner! It would appear as though Catria requires some education in the finer arts of the shovel!"

"Hrm..." Alan muttered. "Then I suppose we should have a duel."

Catria blinked. "What?"

"If I lose, I'll give up my job as Lithisia's bodyguard and leave," he told her.

Catria happily nodded. "And if *I* lose, I'll do whatever you want me to do."

Five minutes later, the two faced one another in combat. Within seconds, Catria's sword was sent flying as if it were nothing more than a piece of trash.

"Sir Miner wins! The shovelscore is now six wins to zero!" Lithisia crowed. The princess was still forcing the word "shovel" into anywhere she deemed suitable, but that wasn't what mattered at the moment.

Catria stared down at her now-empty hand in disbelief. "H-how?! I demand a rematch! Face me one more time!"

"As you wish," Alan replied, handing back her sword.

Catria's blade came swinging down once again, and Alan slowly dodged it. If he moved at full speed, Catria wouldn't have been able to track his movements, and she'd continue to think he was a fraud. To prevent that, he copied the way the bandit leader had moved. The man who had attacked Lithisia on the mountain was far stronger than Catria.

Whoosh, whoosh! The knight's blade connected with nothing but air.

"Urgh...haaah... How are you...?!" Catria panted. She was stunned by the miner's abilities. The man in front of her wasn't just incredibly strong, he was fast. Despite putting her full force and weight into each attack, he barely moved. She felt like an ant facing off against a giant dragon. "This can't be! It's impossible! Who in the hell are you?!"

"I'm a jewel miner."

"Lies! Your movements are those of a knight! A Holy Knight at that! I would know!" Catria's father was a Holy Knight, and this man moved just like him.

"There's no way that's..." Alan trailed off before realizing. *Oh, right.* If he recalled correctly, the bandit leader who attacked Lithisia had said he was a former Holy Knight. Catria had gotten the wrong idea.

"I get it now!" she continued. "I heard of a Holy Knight who retired and went missing! You must be him!"

"...Fine, whatever. I don't even care anymore." It was easier for Alan to just accept that as his new truth. Catria stopped in her tracks.

"So...you're a former Holy Knight...?" Her hands dropped to her sides. After staring at Alan for a time, she slowly took a knee. "I have lost. As promised, you are free to do with me what you will," Catria said, accepting her fate with honor. Her sword dropped to the ground with a *clang*, and she suddenly started to laugh. It was a self-deprecating kind of laugh. "To think that a Holy Knight could be this strong..."

Alan's strength was inhuman. If this was the power that all Holy Knights boasted, then this was the end of the line. She quickly fell into despair. Of course, Catria had no way of knowing that not only was Alan *not* a Holy Knight, he was a miner, and he wasn't even using his full power.

Tears began to form in her eyes.

"Catria! Catria! Hold yourshove together!" Lithisia encouraged her friend.

Alan glared at her. "Okay, you need to back off and be quiet."

"Okey dokey!" Despite going quiet, Lithisia attempted to reach Catria using telepathy. *Hold yourshove together!*

This girl had lost it.

"I'm so sorry, Your Royal Highness. I... I can't..." *I can't live up to your expectations,* Catria wanted to say, but before she could finish her sentence, the ground began to shake. Alan motioned for silence before listening carefully.

"Hrm, more knights are on their way. Thirty this time," he reported.

Catria slowly raised her head. "They're probably looking for me." She cast her gaze to Lithisia, her expression a mystery. She then took hold of her sword, rising from the ground. "Your Royal Highness, this is goodbye. Please stay safe."

"Catria?"

The knight looked as though a great weight had been lifted from her shoulders. "They're after me, so if you run in the opposite direction, you should be safe."

"But what about you?"

Catria smiled brightly. "For someone as untalented as I am, the least I can do is serve as a decoy. I have no regrets." This was the honest truth. She had only just come to realize that her entire life had held no meaning. The thought of throwing her life away no longer seemed crazy to her. "And Sir Holy Knight, might I have your name?"

"I'm not a Holy Knight, but my name is Alan."

"Sir Alan... If you still have any pride left as a Holy Knight, I ask that you swear upon my blade to protect the princess."

"I'm not a knight," he insisted. "Fine...I'll swear on this shovel of mine instead."

"Heh," Catria laughed at his response. "I finally get it. This whole 'shovel' thing you and the princess are doing is just an inside joke to calm your nerves."

Alan rolled his eyes. "If only." He *wished* it was a joke.

Catria held her sword up, her ponytail swaying in the wind. "Sir Alan, I promised you that I would do anything you said, but it looks like I won't be able to keep that promise. Forgive me." As she met his gaze, she realized that this man with incredible strength had been chosen by the heavens.

She had to ask.

"What...what is it that I'm lacking?" Catria whispered.

"Well..." Alan began, but she interrupted him.

"No, you don't have to say anything. I already know. I've always known."

She glanced down at his shovel. Alan had toyed with her like a child with that shovel of his. Even if she trained for a hundred years, she knew for a fact that she'd never clear the bar that Alan had set.

There were some walls that couldn't be overcome by hard work alone. That was what it meant to have talent.

I wasn't chosen.

And just like she hadn't been chosen at birth, the path of the blade did not choose her, either. Catria understood that to a painful degree now.

To her, the man standing in front of her was blindingly bright.

"I...I wanted to be like you." With that confession, the knight turned her back to the man, tears in her eyes, and began to run toward the squad of knights approaching from the hills.

"Now wait just a second!" Alan grabbed her by the collar, stopping her in her tracks.

Catria began to cough after getting grabbed by the neck. "Ack! Wh-what are you doing?! You fool!"

"Don't get ahead of yourself. I can handle thirty knights myself."

"Are you a moron?! You might be a former Holy Knight, but you can't possibly win against those numbers!"

Alan held his shovel up. He had to save this girl. After being dropped into a pit of self-loathing, she was now searching for a place to die.

"Catria. What you lack is not talent."

"Huh?" What was he saying all of a sudden?

"You don't need talent to get stronger." Alan knew this for a fact. "What you need is some mining."

Catria's mouth opened wide. "Huh? Wh-what are you saying...?"

Alan continued his explanation despite Catria's confusion. "Talent isn't just something you find on the ground. It's something you mine from deep within yourself. I don't know much about swordsmanship, but it can't be all that different from shoveling. If you've been training hard like everyone else and you're still weak, that just means you've been mining yourself the wrong way."

"Mining...myself...?"

"So it's time to learn how to mine properly. If you can manage that..." Alan looked Catria straight in the eyes. "You'll become as strong as me. No, even stronger," he declared with certainty.

Catria froze. Lies. This was madness. None of this made any kind of sense. There was no sense to be made! Her mind was screaming at her, yet her heart wouldn't stop racing a mile a minute. After all, he was the strongest man she knew, and he'd stated his words as fact.

I can become as strong as he is?

"You just don't know how to mine yet, and I'm going to prove it to you." Alan gripped his shovel with both hands and held it up high. "Just by mining day in and day out, a simple man like me can do this."

Alan's Shovel Power was increasing. Blue and white energy particles gathered in the area around the shovel at an explosive rate. This was just like when he saved Lithisia, only even more impressive. The shovel's beam was responding to Alan's pure desire to save Catria from her suicidal despair. He pointed the shovel at the knights bearing down on them.

"DIG!" he commanded.

KA-CHOOOOOOOOOOOOOOOMMMMMM!!!!!

A giant beam of light shot out from the shovel at high speed. The power released shook the air, and even felt like it shook the world and maybe even space itself. This was Alan's Wave Motion Shovel Blast, and there was no way that a human or a horse could survive the same force that had pierced an entire mountain. The thirty approaching knights, as well as the fortress behind them, vanished into a blinding flash of light.

"Yaaaay!" Lithisia cheered. "You did it, Sir Miner! What a shovely amazing Wave Motion Shovel Blast!"

"Don't act so surprised. It's not like you haven't seen this before, Lithisia."

Then it hit her. "Oh, but you killed all those knights..." She lowered her head. "Rest in peace," she said.

"I've killed no one. I changed the beam's attribute to 'bury'. They and their horses can be dug up and saved."

"Amazing! You buried the horses, too?! Your sense of humor is shovely wonderful!"

Alan decided to let that go for now. He turned back toward Catria, who was standing in stunned silence. She must've finally understood what "mining" meant. "If you learn to mine properly, you too can tap into that power!" he said with confidence.

Time passed slowly, but finally Catria began to tremble. "I... I can do that...?"

She clenched her shaking fists. A moment passed.

And then something snapped inside of her.

"THERE'S NO WAY I COULD EVER DO SOMETHING LIKE THAAAAAAT!!!!!" Catria screamed to the heavens.

That was how Catria came to travel alongside Alan and Lithisia.

"This makes no sense! Your shovel makes no sense!" She was still trying to make head or tail of Alan's weird powers as the three of them dug up the ground, freeing the unconscious knights and horses.

"What about it doesn't make sense?"

"Normal shovels don't shoot beams! That's a fact!"

Normal this, normal that, Alan thought. *Nobles are sure hung up on "normal."*

"Mrrghh...nonsense! Mining? Talent? All just complete nonsense!" Catria grumbled. Despite her words, she couldn't help but grin slightly, a tiny spark of hope growing inside her as she considered Alan's explanation. As for the miner himself, he decided that he had to mine as much talent out of this girl as possible.

"By the way, Lithisia. What's our next destination?"

"Well, since the fortress is gone and it's safe now, let's find a place to stay the night...oh." Lithisia had just realized something important. "Stay...stay the night..." She hid her face with her red shovel. "U-um, I'm so sorry for the other night. So, um..."

"What is it?"

"If you're not still upset, maybe tonight..." Lithisia had strengthened her resolve as much as possible, despite her fidgeting about. "We could practice 'shoveling' together?"

"Uh, sure, why not?"

The princess' face lit up. "Thank you so much! I'll do my best!" Lithisia bowed. *I said it! I can't believe I said something shovely daring!*

She was clearly nervous about something, but Alan decided to ignore it for the time being. After all, he already knew that the princess was a weirdo, so what was there to be concerned about?

"I-I'm gonna shovel lots and lots!"

...well, besides how badly each kept misinterpreting the other.

PART 6
Lithisia's Training Shovel

THAT NIGHT, Catria—who was familiar with the area—guided the group to an inn at a small town near the border. While still in front of the building, Catria decided to shoot straight with the miner.

"Sir Alan, just for the record, I still don't trust you. However, it appears that Her Royal Highness does...so let's just say I'm watching you very carefully."

"I appreciate that. I'm looking forward to working with you, Lady Knight."

"...Wh-what's with the whole 'nice guy' act? I've got my eye on you. I'm not here to be friends," the knight responded, her cheeks growing warm. Despite her words, she was just a wee bit happy that he was treating her like a knight.

Lithisia looked around inside the building. "So this is an inn? Wow, they even have alcohol!" The princess wasn't wearing her usual outfit, but rather a well-tailored one-piece. She looked like the daughter of a wealthy family. Her long blonde hair had been cut short. According to the princess, this transformation ability was one of the abilities possessed by her "Prismatica Dress".

"Its power is all charged up, so I can transform my clothes into any disguise I want."

"You can even change your hair? That's nuts. I bet that thing must be really useful." Alan surmised that her magical dress was likely what helped her escape the capital.

"Useful...?" Lithisia tilted her head as the miner stood by, impressed. "Ah!" The princess' cheeks turned bright red and she cast her gaze at the floor. "Y-yes, um, it can transform into all kinds of clothes... I imagine it'll be quite useful to you, Sir Miner..."

She was acting odd again, but this was nothing new. "So how are we splitting the rooms?"

"Two were available. Rooms 205 and 206," Catria answered.

"Then Sir Miner and I will take 205, and you can have 206," Lithisia replied with a smile.

"...Um, excuse me, Your Royal Highness, but is your brain still filled with shovels?"

"C-Catria, how dare you say something so rude to your princess?!"

"No, I think Catria picked the right words," Alan added. "There's no way the two of us are sharing the same room. You can stay with Catria."

"Thank goodness. I'm glad you're a man of sense, Sir Alan."

"Huh?!" Lithisia shouted in surprise. "B-but Sir Miner, didn't you promise me we'd practice 'shoveling' together?!"

"Shoveling practice?" What did she mean by "shoveling" this time? The word had taken on so many different meanings in her head that it was impossible to decide which one she meant at any given time. "I assume you mean making a sign, yeah?" Alan figured that posting signs at village inns and taverns would be useful in letting the townsfolk know that he was looking for an apprentice.

"Huh? U-um, no, I mean the one where we work, um, together."

"Oh, so you mean getting down and dirty, then?" By which Alan meant actually digging into the dirt, of course.

"Down and dirty?!" the princess repeated, by which she did *not* mean digging into the dirt. She began to fidget and her cheeks turned pink as she made a few embarrassed little noises. "Y-yes, um...I'm certain we'll be exerting lots of energy together..." Lithisia nodded.

Alan decided that Lithisia was definitely referring to the act of digging. "Got it. Perfect timing. I noticed a lovely little garden around the inn, so we'll work there."

"In the garden? Um, outside?!"

"Huh...? Why're you so surprised? Shovels are usually used outside."

"What...? 'Shoveling' is done *outside*?!" Lithisia's eyes were darting all over. She looked like a cat tracking a small flying insect. "I'm so ignorant..." she moaned. For some reason, her breathing had become rough and uneven. "I see... Doing it outside is normal for you..." She straightened. "All right! Th-then I'll do my best outside!"

"How does nine tonight sound? Make sure you wear something easy to move in."

"O-okay! I'll take a bath and clean myself off first!"

"Uh...you should probably hold off on the bath until afterward."

"O-oh, yes. I suppose we will be getting dirty in all kinds of ways!"

Lithisia was acting suspicious again, but again Alan thought nothing of it. If anything, this had become her normal way of acting since they began their journey.

Time passed, and eventually the two met up in the garden.

"Sir Miner, I-I'm here."

Alan turned at the sound of her voice. "Great, I've been waiting for—*whoa*!"

Beneath the pale moonlight was Lithisia, looking like she was wearing some kind of student uniform. It was the sort of formal uniform one would expect from a child of nobility. However, her thighs were exposed, tightly pressed together below the hem of her skirt, and she was wearing white knee socks. The miniskirt she wore was impossibly short. If she moved even a little bit, he'd be able to see what lay beneath it.

"A-ah..." Upon noticing Alan's gaze, she pulled the hem of her skirt down, embarrassed. She then immediately stopped upon realizing that she should probably let Alan look as much as he wanted. "Um, so this is the uniform I wore at the Royal Academy..." Lithisia explained as she squirmed about. "What do you think, Sir Miner?"

"...What do I think?"

"Yes. If you're going to teach me how to 'shovel,' that would make me your student."

"Hrm, I see." For once, Lithisia's awful sense made... sense. "It's all fine and dandy that you're dressed the part, but isn't that skirt a little too short?" It was, in fact, *amazingly* short.

"Ah, um, yes. It's two-thirds shorter than the norm, actually."

"Why?!"

Lithisia averted her gaze, embarrassed again. "I thought it'd be easier to 'shovel' if it was short…" Her face turned bright red, as if she were on the verge of exploding.

"But if you work in that, I'll be able to see your panties." If Alan had to be perfectly honest, he didn't think a fifteen-year-old should be dressing this way at all.

"Yes, but, um, I'm prepared!" Lithisia stated, her voice trembling. It was true that a long skirt would simply get in the way. At the end of the day, all was well…provided Alan didn't look. "Oh! Or should I have just come naked?!"

"Naked?!" *Why?!* "No, no. Wearing clothes is a must."

"Really? I always thought doing it in the nude was standard practice."

"Absolutely not! Clothes are vital to this kind of activity. Never forget that."

"O-o-o-okay! I won't!" Lithisia held her red shovel up to her breasts and breathed in and out to steady herself. "So doing it clothed and outside is the norm? Wow, 'shoveling' sure is complex!"

Lithisia and Alan were thinking in completely opposite directions, but neither she nor the miner had yet realized it.

Alan sat Lithisia down, and as a result, the miner could almost see under her skirt, so he used his orichalcum-tier self-restraint to look away. "Let's get started. Watch me carefully."

"Yes, Sir Miner... Please teach me everything you know..."

Ignoring Lithisia's strangely aroused tone, Alan began to swing his shovel. Lithisia nearly closed her eyes but thought better of it. She had to watch. Sir Miner was going out of his way to practice with her. He was going to teach her all about 'shoveling.' Both her mind and heart would become one with the shovel. *I have to memorize everything,* she vowed, *no matter how embarrassing it is!*

Before her very eyes, the miner's shovel dug into the ground.

"Huh?"

This wasn't a metaphor for something lewd. Alan was actually digging up dirt.

"Hrm, this is some good soil," Alan said. He continued to dig up the dirt at his feet. He thrust the red shovel into the ground, lifted the soil, and repeated the process over and over again. The repetition was fundamental to shoveling, since one couldn't just shovel all the dirt in one go. The key was having the physical stamina to keep going.

"Um, er..."

"What's wrong? Have a question?"

"It looks like you're just digging up dirt..."

"Of course. This is the cycle of shoveling. The very basics. Repeatedly digging up dirt."

"The basics... The basics... Ah, I get it!" Lithisia's eyes shone brightly. "I understand at last!"

"What, exactly?"

"Digging up dirt uses the same motion required for 'shoveling'!"

At this point, Lithisia's misunderstanding had grown so large that it eclipsed the largest mountain on the planet.

"In other words, the ground is me, and the shovel is Sir Miner's...um, 'shovel'...!" The princess cast her gaze at the earth, her cheeks red.

"I have no idea what you're talking about, but whatever. Digging up dirt repeatedly is where it all starts. Here." Alan positioned himself behind the girl. Practice made perfect, after all.

"Eh? Oh, doing it repeatedly... Ah, you're so rough... aaah!"

For some reason, Lithisia seemed embarrassed as she averted her gaze. Each time the shovel stabbed into the dirt, she made all kinds of moans, her ample breasts jiggling and her legs lifting her skirt ever higher. Alan was on the verge of peeking where he really shouldn't, but instead he firmly closed his mind off and just continued to dig.

"Aaah. *Aaahh...*"

Lithisia's cheeks were flaming, and she was clenching her thighs tightly together like she was holding something back. She continued to fidget this way over and over again. Perhaps she had concerns about how to move the shovel?

"Oh, and it's important to put strength into your thrusts."

"H-huh?! You mean you're not gentle?" Lithisia held herself tightly. What was she protecting herself from?

"This is important. I know it might be difficult because of your figure, but hang in there."

"Aaaaaaaaaah!" Lithisia shrunk into herself, looking even more embarrassed than she did when their lesson started. After a moment, however, a look of determination crossed her face. "I...I understand! I'll be fine no matter how rough it gets!"

"That's my girl. You especially have to be careful when the dirt changes."

It took several seconds before Lithisia responded. "Huh? You mean the dirt might change?"

"Of course."

"You mean it'll be someone else, not me?!" Lithisia began to actively sob.

"Why are you crying?! Are you hurt?!"

"No, I-I'm sorry... You're right... Catria is beautiful, after all..."

"What does she have to do with you crying?!"

Lithisia stopped in her tracks. "So...so right now, um... the only dirt you're digging is what's right here?"

"I have no clue where you're going with this, but yes. I mean, there'll certainly be more dirt to dig elsewhere in the future."

The expression on Lithisia's face softened. After a few seconds of thinking about it, she spoke up softly. "I...I'm going to practice all the things you taught me today, Sir Miner."

"I'm so confused right now, but uh, good luck?"

"So, um, in the future, even if the dirt is different..." Lithisia brought her hands together tightly in front of her chest as if she was praying. "I hope you always remember this dirt..." The princess looked up at Alan as if she were wishing upon the stars. "It doesn't have to be all the time, but I hope that, from time to time, you remember the first dirt you dug up... It'd make me happy."

Alan took a deep breath and stared up helplessly at the moon. He was at his limit. He had absolutely no idea what Lithisia was talking about. What did she *want* from him? *Even so...she seems completely serious.* He could tell that much with one look at her eyes. He decided to answer just as seriously. "From time to time? Psh. I *never* forget the dirt I've dug up."

Her feelings reached a fever pitch, and Lithisia began to cry again, tears falling onto her school uniform. "Sir Miner...!"

"And remember, I'm a jewel miner. I keep digging in one place until I find what I'm looking for."

Lithisia was sweating profusely for some reason. "What you're looking for? My gosh...!" One thought and one thought alone echoed in her head:

Sir Miner, I wub you!

"All right, that's that. Let's continue practicing," Alan said.

"Of course! Thank you very much!"

And so they continued to dig.

"Aaah! Nnngh! Not there! It's so rough! Aaaaah!"

With every bit of dirt dug up, the princess continued to make strange noises and twist her body about, but Alan ignored her. Eventually dawn broke.

The pair's fatal misunderstanding had only grown worse.

The next morning, Alan and the others left the inn and were once again on their way.

"Your Royal Highness, we're about to enter the Elf Woods soon."

"Wubby... <3."

"It's a dangerous place. If possible, I'd like to avoid... Er, Your Royal Highness? "

"Wubby dubby... <3"

"Catria, what's wrong with Lithisia?"

"I know not. Did you do something to her last night?"

"Not at all. We just dug up some dirt together with our shovels."

"I know. I was watching the two of you."

"I wubby my shovely... <3"

The princess was getting on Catria's last nerve. She shook her head from side to side, trying to restrain herself. *No, no. The princess saved my life. I have to protect her, no matter what.* She clenched her fists. *Even if she's become...that!*

Even Catria had begun referring to Lithisia's madness as "that."

CHAPTER 2

The Grassland Nation's Shovel
(FIORIEL'S INTRODUCTION)

THE INVINCIBLE
SHOVEL

PART 7
The Miner Becomes Fioriel's Uncle

THE ELF WOODS stretched out far and wide before the party. The massive forest had existed long before the nations of men came into existence on this continent, back during the age of legends and fairy tales. This was where the long-eared demi-humans known as elves had lived...once upon a time.

"I heard from Gramps that the elves had gone extinct," Lithisia explained at the entrance to the forest. "During the War of Genocide hundreds of years ago, the demon king not only managed to kill half of humanity with his army, he also annihilated the elves. To the demons, this forest was something like a hunting ground. All kinds of beasts snuck in and ate the remaining elves."

Alan had spent hundreds of years beneath the surface, so to him, this was brand-new information. "How unfortunate..." he said. "I would have loved to meet an elf in person."

"Why is that?" Catria asked him, but Lithisia jumped in instead.

"Elves and shovels. Elves and shovels... They just kinda feel like they go together!" Lithisia explained proudly.

Wait, what? the miner thought, confused. "Well, either way, we have to get through here. Don't worry, I once got permission from the elf elder to come and go as I please."

"Excuse me? The elf elder?" Catria questioned the miner. "You make it sound like you were pals."

"We were. I was the one who got the elder the Blaze Ruby that sealed away the Great Spirit Ifrit."

"The Great Spirit Ifrit? No way. When did that supposedly happen?"

"Hm, about three hundred... No, it was 420 years ago."

"Wha—?"

"Yup! Sir Miner is actually 1,011 years old!" Lithisia giggled. She still didn't seem to believe him.

"The Elf Woods are dangerous, but fear not. You see..." Alan held up his shovel. "The shovel shines brightest when used to explore vast forests."

"Shoveltastic!"

"...Somebody please explain to me how a shovel could be useful in a forest? Actually, no, don't." Catria knew all that awaited her was another mystifying answer.

Alan motioned for the ladies to stay. "Wait here. I'm going to check on ahead."

"Ah, Sir Miner! Please wait!" Lithisia drew close to Alan.

He was unsure of what she was thinking as she stabbed her red shovel into the dirt. She then took a knee next to it and looked up at him.

"May the Great Shovel God be with you," she whispered.

An uncomfortable few moments passed. "...What just happened?" Alan knew better than to ask, but he did so anyway.

Lithisia giggled with a smile on her face. "It's my country's new religion! God exists everywhere, right? Therefore, God exists within the shovel."

Silence set over the forest. At what point exactly had this nutty princess created a completely new religion? Alan shook his head. "I should have never asked."

"As far as naming goes, I'd like to keep it nice and simple: the Holy Shovel Faith. And I would be its high priestess!"

"You've completely lost me." Alan was now certain that Lithisia had been entirely corrupted by the very concept of the shovel.

"I'm just having trouble coming up with a phrase of blessing. 'Scoop' feels a bit cheap, don't you think?"

"Please don't ask me."

"Maybe we should go with something like 'Dig' or 'Alan'?"

"Seriously, don't ask me." Alan looked at Catria. "Look, you handle the princess. I'll be back by nightfall."

"What?! W-wait, what do you expect me to do?!" Catria sputtered.

"Sir Miner, take care! Alan!" Lithisia made the sign of the cross in the air with her shovel. Alan paid her no mind and entered the forest.

⊳─────▶

Upon entering the Elf Woods, Alan noticed something strange.

The trees were twisted out of shape and had turned purple. In fact, they were pulsating creepily, as if they were undead flora. This was nothing like the vibrant Elf Woods of Alan's memory. The river water had been corrupted by the black liquid streaming from the trees. All of this served as proof that the elves really were no more.

What happened to this place?

Alan held up his shovel and used its "Shovel Search" ability. He'd learned this technique in Layer #103 of the mountain, the Underground Sea of Trees. It allowed him to locate the origins of water, places where the liquid had gathered, and also ascertain the liquid's quality. All he had to do was focus his power into the head of the shovel. Same old, same old.

"Hrm...there's still a clean spring left," he muttered. Just then, he heard the sound of water splashing from beyond the trees. Was it an animal of some sort? He had a bad feeling about this.

Alan quickly ran through the forest and came out beyond the shadows of the large trees. "Who's there?!"

"Oh!" came a startled voice.

"...Huh?" Alan looked at the figure standing in the spring.

It was a girl. She almost looked like the spirit of the spring. She had a beautiful, slender body, and the water came up to around her knees. Water dripped from her shoulder-length blonde hair. The girl was completely nude, which meant that Alan could see everything. When she turned to face him, her breasts jiggled.

The girl's body was perfectly mature, despite her young face. The light of the moon reflected off of her beautiful skin.

"Eh…? Aaaaaah!!!" The girl immediately covered her breasts and began to scream. At the sides of her surprised face were two pointy ears. She was an elf! "Don't look! Wh-who are you?!"

Alan finally realized that he was peeping at a young elf girl as she tried to bathe. This was bad. He had to apologize. Of course, first he had to stop staring. Just as the gears in his brain began to turn, his shovel started vibrating.

It sensed something. The enemy from earlier!

"Run!" Alan shouted at the elf girl.

"Huh?!"

Alan leapt into the air just as a four-legged beast came flying toward them from out of nowhere. He recognized the creature. It was a powerful Dark Beast from the Dark World, and it was aiming for the elf girl, its fangs shining in the light.

"What?! A beast?!" The elf girl panicked but nonetheless quickly moved her hands. She was clearly trying to use Spirit Magic.

But Alan and his shovel were faster. "DIG!" he commanded. The Dark Beast was flattened against the ground with a roaring *KA-CHOOOOOOM!* But Alan didn't stop there. He pushed the creature further down, shoving it beneath the ground, until it had been completely covered with soil.

"What..." said the elf girl in shock. "What just happened?"

"I buried it," Alan replied.

"You *what*?"

Alan explained that a shovel could do two things: It could dig things up, and it could bury them. By hacking into an enemy's body, Alan could kill them. By burying them, he could seal them under the ground. He'd gone with the latter for the Dark Beast. He called this technique "Shovel Sealing."

"More importantly, are you all right?" he asked the girl. "Did you get any blood on you?"

"Uh...no, I'm fine." The elf girl raised both hands and examined her moist body. "I don't have a mark on me... Oh, excuse me! Thank you so much!"

She politely bowed her head. Her golden blonde hair was stuck to her beautiful skin.

"I'm sorry," Alan said. "I have my eyes closed, so could you put on some clothes?"

"Huh? Clothes...? Oh! Oh my gosh!" The young girl finally remembered that she was in the buff. She quickly covered her private bits with her hands.

"I-I-I'm so sorry! I'm so sorry you had to see me like this!"

"No, no, you don't need to apologize," Alan said quickly. "You're quite beautiful."

"Eep!" The elf girl gave a little shriek, and tried to curl herself up into a ball.

The miner probably could have chosen his words better.

After she'd dressed, the elf girl implored the miner to let her express her gratitude, so he allowed himself to be led to her home. She led Alan deep within the woods to a small cabin made from a hollowed-out tree. It seemed like the demons and beasts hadn't encroached this far into the woodland.

"Mr. Human, thank you very much for saving me," said the elf girl as she lifted her teapot and poured some tea into Alan's cup. Judging by the way her pointy ears twitched, she was clearly glad just to have company. "My name is Fioriel. It's a bit of a mouthful, so you can call me Fio." She had a very calm and tranquil air about her, apparently no longer bothered by having been seen in the nude earlier.

"I didn't think there were any elves left," Alan said. "Are you alone?"

"Well..." Fio looked down at the floor. It didn't take much for Alan to guess at her situation. The strange presence he felt when he entered the forest, the Dark Beast from earlier... The young elf girl was the last of her kind. If anything, she should be praised for surviving at all.

"Do you have any means to protect yourself?"

"Yes. I know a little Spirit Magic. Branch Slash, it's called."

"Oh, you can wield Spirit Magic? Impressive."

Fio's expression darkened. "No... I'm a failure of a Spirit Mage... A failure of an elf..."

"Huh...?" Alan was puzzled. Fio had reacted swiftly to the attacking beast from earlier. It was clear that she had undergone training. If anything, it was safe to say that as a Spirit Mage, she was quite adept.

"S-so, um, Mr. Human... May I have your name?" Apparently not wanting to continue down this line of conversation, Fio changed the subject.

"Ah, my apologies. I'm Alan. Alan the jewel miner."

"Alan...?" Fio tilted her head. "Why does that name sound so familiar...?"

"I've been to the elf village before. Maybe that's why."

"Huh?!" the elf girl raised her voice in surprise.

"At the time, I gave a jewel to Elder Pasarunak as a gift."

"Pasarunak?!" Fio gasped. "You knew him?"

"Yes. Do you?"

Fio's eyes were shining. "Elder Pasarunak, King of the Silver Tree... He's my ancestor!" She looked at the miner carefully. "Wait, Sir Alan... Does that mean y-you're the legendary Old Digger?!"

"Most likely."

"O-oh my gosh! This is incredible! You're the man from the book!" Fio was so happy that she was jumping up and down, her breasts bouncing along with the rest of her body. Alan had no clue where to look, but eventually settled upon her face. She did resemble Pasarunak in some ways.

"Then that'd make you his descendant, eh? Man, that takes me back."

"Um, er, but..." Fio looked down at the ground as though she wasn't sure what to say. "Um... I know I said Pasarunak is my ancestor and all, but..."

"What's wrong?"

"I think, well, this part of my body is..." Embarrassed, Fio gestured at her extremely buxom chest. "...a little big for an elf, isn't it?"

Fio brought her breasts together tightly, an action that was nearly impossible to look away from. Her chest was so big that Alan felt magnetically drawn to them. If she lived in a human village, men and women alike would constantly be trying to woo her.

"I mean, I guess in some ways you could describe them as weird...but, uh, I quite like them," Alan admitted.

"Huh?" Fio exclaimed.

Alan immediately tried to correct himself. "I don't mean that in a perverted way!" He was unsure of how to phrase his words. After thinking for a moment, he decided to just be honest with the girl. "I don't know how elven standards of beauty work, but I think you're, um, quite cute."

"Cute?!" she repeated in shock.

"Yeah. Speaking as a human, I think you're extremely cute. I bet there are men all over the place who wish they could make you their wife."

"Wife?!" Fio was flustered as she looked at her body, then back at his. Her cheeks turned bright red and she quickly averted her gaze. "Um, I-I'm sorry! I'm so sorry!"

Why is she apologizing?

"A-anyway, um, regardless of whether I'm cute or not, I don't have the body of an elf."

"Well, sure."

"That's why, um, I think that I might not be related to him by blood."

"That can't be," Alan immediately replied. "The color of your eyes, the shape of your ears... You look just like Pasarunak."

"Huh?!"

"I can guarantee it. You are definitely his descendant."

Fio was speechless as she stared at Alan. "E-excuse me, I... Really? I look like him...?" She closed her eyes and brought her arms together.

Alan could tell that she was truly moved by his words, but he was a bit puzzled. "Fio, do you really trust me that easily?"

"What do you mean?"

"Don't you find it odd that I'm saying I knew Pasarunak personally?" He had met the legendary elder some four hundred years ago. Most people wouldn't believe that sort of tale. Catria certainly hadn't, and even Lithisia thought he was bluffing. Nobody actually believed Alan was *that* old.

"Huh? But..." Fio tilted her head, befuddled. "You're the Old Digger, are you not?"

"I am," he nodded.

"Then, um, there's nothing odd about it." Fio was legitimately confused by his question, like she hadn't been taught to doubt. Despite Alan having seen her naked, she hadn't been angry with him, either. Considering how she'd lived alone in the woods all this time, she was probably even more naive about the ways of the world than Lithisia. The princess had received a proper education due to her position as royalty, but Fio likely had no one to teach her anything.

Although, Alan thought, Lithisia had gone off the deep end as of late, so maybe he shouldn't compare the two.

"Um, Sir Alan? Could you tell me more about yourself and Lord Pasarunak?"

She wanted to know about her great ancestor. Alan nodded his head. "Sure. let me tell you about the time he greeted me with a 'World Tree Cocktail'."

Alan ended up telling Fio all kinds of old stories. The elf girl listened quietly and intently to every word he had to say, but the tale that got the biggest reaction out of her was when he told her about how Pasarunak once offered to marry his little sister off to the miner.

"Oh my gosh! That's amazing! Amazing!" She just couldn't stop using the word *amazing*. "Sir Alan, had things been different, you might have ended up living here in the forest…"

"Yeah, but I'm a miner at heart, so…"

The little sister in question had looked every bit as beautiful as Fio would be when she grew older. Now that Alan thought about it, that young woman was likely Fio's ancestor as well. If he was being truly honest, he had been tremendously attracted to Pasarunak's little sister. But if he had taken a wife and had a child in the Elf Woods, he wouldn't have been able to go digging around the mountain. He'd ended up declining the offer and returned to the depths from whence he came.

"I should have waited a little longer before heading back..." Alan muttered to himself. He thought about the forest's current condition. It was clear to him that the Elf Woods were dying. If he'd stayed here, he would never have let things get this bad. "Are the Dark Beasts to blame for the undead state of the forest?"

Fio was hesitant to answer, but nonetheless nodded. "Those beasts are the servants of the Devil. They corrupt the trees and the water wherever they settle...and they're what killed all the other elves."

Alan didn't need to hear anything else. "Got it. Give me some time." The miner grabbed his shovel and stood up. He was about to leave before Fio panicked and grabbed his arm.

"Um, what are you planning to do, Sir Alan?!"

"I'm going to crush the Dark Beasts."

Fio's jaw dropped. "N-no! You can't!" Fio grasped his arm more firmly, desperately trying to stop him. "You can't! You absolutely cannot! You'll be killed!"

"I'll be fine. I'm pretty strong."

"I-I know you are, but the beasts are endless!"

"That's fine. I've got infinite shovel powers."

"Infinite shovel powers?!" *What the heck are those?!* Fio thought. She tightened her grip. "P-please, I beg of you! It's too dangerous!"

The tears began to fall from her eyes. Alan couldn't just brush her off, so he decided to explain himself. "But Fio, if I don't defeat the Dark Beasts, this forest is doomed."

The elf girl didn't know what to say. "But, but... There's no reason for you to put yourself in danger, Sir Alan."

"You're wrong. There is a reason."

"Huh?"

"You're a descendent of Pasarunak, which means you're basically family." He may have turned down the marriage proposal, but he was forever recognized as a friend to the elves. That meant Fio was his friend, and someone who fell under his protection. "I mean, if I'd married the elder's sister, you would have been my niece."

"Your niece?!"

"Mmm-hmm. Feel free to call me 'Uncle Alan' if you want."

"U-Uncle Alan...?!"

Fio had a huge smile on her face despite her shock. *Uncle.* The human who saved her life, the legendary Old Digger...Uncle Alan. It had a beautiful ring to it. Fioriel was, at long last, no longer alone in the world.

"Ah!" Fio shook her head back and forth. "N-no! You can't! I mean, I... I...." Her expression hardened. "I don't n-need you to eliminate the beasts."

"You don't?"

"No, I don't! I mean..." Fio cast her gaze out of the window. Outside was a beautiful field of flowers. A spring was nearby, its crystal waters glittering in the light. "There's an ancient energy barrier around the house that keeps the beasts out."

She wasn't lying. Alan could feel traces of holy power in the area.

"Plus, I'm the only elf left. I live here on my own, so there's no reason for someone to defeat the Dark Beasts." Fio clenched her fists tightly. "Uncle Alan, I, um, don't need your help." The elf girl flashed him a radiant smile— one that was obviously forced.

Which was why Alan made his decision. "You're a liar," he said bluntly.

"Huh?!" Her smile collapsed in an instant. "No, I'm not!"

"Then why are you crying?"

Fio froze. "Um, uh...I-I'm just sweating! Elves sweat from their eyes!"

There was no talking her way out of this. Regardless of how she tried to spin things, she was in tears. Should he stop pushing the subject? He briefly considered the option before tossing it out. In order to help Fio, he needed to know why she was so insistent on rejecting his help.

He also had to know why the elf girl was crying those jewel-like tears. After all, Alan was a jewel miner. Digging up precious jewels was his entire reason for being.

"Fio. You're gonna explain to me why you're crying. Here, use this shovel."

"...Huh?" Fio wasn't sure what Alan was getting at as he turned the handle of his shovel toward her. More accurately, he turned his shovel to her past. By offering the shovel to her, he would be able to unearth her past the same way he'd unearthed all manner of precious things.

In other words, it was a "Time Shovel."

"DIG!" he commanded.

A booming noise shook the cabin, and just like that, Alan had dug up Fio's past.

A translucent double of Fio was seated at the nearby table. She seemed a bit younger than the flesh-and-blood elf girl with Alan, whose jaw had dropped in shock. "H-Huh?!" she gasped.

The transparent Fio spoke. "Hey, hey, Dine, um, I got stronger!" she said excitedly to a water spirit nearby. "If I keep it up, maybe one day I'll be able to defeat the Dark Beasts!"

"...Yeah, maybe," the spirit replied. "It'll be really, really hard, though."

"But I'm going to do my best!" Past Fio said. "I've made my decision, and once I chase the Dark Beasts out, the forest will come back to life! Then...I'm sure the elves who are living somewhere else will come back."

Past Fio raised her head and looked out the window at what the village of elves once looked like. There was a shrine made of some kind of white tree, and in the public square, elves sang and danced. Past Fio smiled. "I'm sure they'll become my friends!"

> ⊶───▶

The vision ended there, and Fio was reduced to a mess of tears. Alan had forced her to confront her painful past—the dream she'd given up on.

It was some time before Fio spoke again.

"I... I couldn't do it." She took a shaky breath. "I tried to fight the Dark Beasts, and I lost... Dine bought me time to flee..."

It was then that she lost her only friend, the water spirit.

"There isn't just one beast..." Fio gripped Alan's wrist once more. "Dozens... Hundreds... Thousands... Their numbers are beyond comprehension." Her voice was trembling. It was the voice of someone who had experienced horrific things first-hand. "So it's impossible. I can't do it anymore."

Fio looked up at Alan. The look in her eyes was familiar. *Catria's eyes looked the same way in the pit, just before she tried to...* He didn't have a chance to finish the thought before Fio spoke up again.

"Please. I'm serious. Please don't go."

Both women's eyes held the pain of one who was facing an insurmountable wall and had fallen into despair. Both had had dreams that were shattered into pieces.

"I can't take any more friends dying because of my mistakes..."

Several moments passed. Alan considered his words carefully. "Fio, you're just like me," he finally told her. "You're a miner."

"What?" Fio wasn't following, but Alan was certain of it.

Fio was absolutely a miner. Ordinary miners dug holes into the ground to look for jewels. In Fio's case, her jewels were called "friends," and the way she delved for them was by using Spirit Magic to drive the Dark Beasts from the forest. What else was she if not a miner?

"Which means it's my responsibility to help you."

"Uncle Alan!" Fio panicked, but the miner simply smiled.

"Don't worry. I have an idea." The Dark Beasts rose endlessly from the depths, but Alan knew the depths of the earth better than anyone. He'd already come up with a plan to deal with these creatures. "My shovel can handle this."

Fio was completely taken aback. "Huh? Your shovel...? What are you saying, Uncle Alan?!"

There was a certain type of structure Alan had built numerous times during the Jewel War as a barrier against the dragons and demons. He glanced out the window to guess at the time. The sun hadn't set yet, so he still had plenty of time. He decided to get right to work.

"I'm going to build an elf castle right here," the miner stated simply.

Thus was the origin of what would later be referred to as the legendary "Overnight Elven Castle."

PART 8
The Miner Constructs an Elf Castle

THIRTY SECONDS was all it took for Alan to eliminate the Dark Beasts.

Fio was appalled by the utter lack of logic implicit in that feat. "Wait, Uncle Alan! This makes no sense!"

"What about it doesn't make sense?" Alan replied from the center of the opening in the forest. At his feet was a mountain of Dark Beast corpses piled on top of one another. He would later use Shovel Fire to burn the bodies, and Holy Shovel to purify the area.

But Fio's eyes were darting all over the place. "E-everything! H-how could you have defeated the Dark Beasts in seconds?"

It had taken only one attack for Alan to eliminate the creatures that caused Fio so much despair. She had no idea what had happened.

"It's the power of the shovel."

"The power of the shovel..."

Fio seemed satisfied with the answer, but in reality, she'd just given up on trying to comprehend what had transpired before her very eyes. He placed a scroll on the table and undid it, revealing a map with a number of squares and circles drawn on it.

"This is the plan for the elf castle," he told her.

Fio continued repeating "the power of the shovel" to herself, completely bewildered. She didn't even notice that Alan had changed the subject.

"Are you okay with me using the 'Fire Knoll' design from four hundred years ago?" he asked her. Fio was clearly not okay in any sense of the word, but Alan nonetheless took her silence as a yes. He immediately began drafting up a schedule for completing the large building. He'd be handling both the interior and exterior design, so he estimated that it would take him about two hours.

"Excuse me, Uncle Alan..." Fio interjected. "But are you sure that estimate is correct?"

"Yeah. Two hours is right."

Fio began to question her sanity. She then spoke up again. "Um, pardon me, but I have a question. What exactly do you plan on making in two hours?"

"An elf castle. The plan is for it to be seven floors tall."

"The castles I'm familiar with can't be built in two hours. Building one should take over two years."

"Needless to say, I do have to make some adjustments."

"Adjustments?" Fio repeated.

"No worries. I'm a miner and a pro. Just trust me."

Jewel miners were essentially extremely talented underground architects. Creating cabins, ladders, and tools for the job was part of their work. Mining a large mountain wasn't just about digging into the ground.

It was time for Alan to show his true skill as a miner.

"I, um, believe in you, Uncle Alan, but..." she trailed off.

Alan interpreted that as permission to begin construction. "Building a trench to defend against invaders is one of the fundamentals of any castle project. So first, I'm going to dig a trench around the Elf Woods."

The Elf Woods, incidentally, had a radius of a little over thirty miles. Fio felt the need to point out the obvious. "I'm sorry, but I can't help but think this plan might have a few...holes in it," she said as gently as possible.

"I suppose you're right," Alan said. "If my shovel wasn't made of adamantine, it'd be impossible."

"Does the shovel quality matter?"

"If it isn't tough enough, it'll break midway through construction."

Alan got to work. Using his Construct Power, he dug a hole around the forest while his shovel emitted a blue and white aura. The hole was about three hundred feet deep and fifteen feet wide. The castle walls themselves would be about sixty feet tall, preventing Dark Beasts from leaping over them. In addition to that, he installed a guardrail to make sure that Fio wouldn't fall into the trench. It was a surprising amount of work, but at Mach One, it took Alan ten whole minutes to create a guardrail that ran around all thirty miles of the Elf Woods.

Shortly thereafter, he and Fio were back in her cabin. She offered him some black tea as if in a daze. "Uncle Alan, am...am I dreaming right now?" she asked as she poured the tea.

"You're not dreaming. This is reality, Fio. If you want proof, think about how delicious this tea is."

"B-but...it's all so *strange*!"

"You keep saying things like that. What's so strange?"

"There's almost too much to list."

"Hrm." Alan looked at the castle wall that stretched on beyond the horizon and mulled it over. It never hurt to get an outside opinion on one's work. Obviously, there had to be some truth to her words. It was up to him to find what that truth was. Suddenly, he snapped his fingers. "Got it! I see now! You're right, Fio. This *is* strange!"

"Y-you finally understand?!"

Alan nodded firmly. "There's no bridge!"

Words could not describe the expression on Fio's face.

"I see now..." he went on. "Since I can use my Shovel Hook to attach a wire to the castle walls and hoist myself over them, I completely failed to consider the necessity of a bridge. I'm so sorry; of course you'd need one. Give me a moment and I'll build one in a jiffy."

Fio didn't need a bridge. Fio didn't need anything except for her uncle to make sense. Her expression was steady, but she was weeping inside.

Alan took his time constructing the bridge. He realized that it'd be hard for Fio to maintain on her own, so he'd have to make it especially sturdy. He decided to utilize arches for sturdiness. Usually it took him no more than three seconds to finish a similar job, but this one took him a whopping three minutes. Ten bridges total meant half an hour overall.

Of course, Alan remembered to include checkpoints at the entrance to each bridge. He equipped them with auto-sensors, granting passage only to those whom Fio recognized.

"Perfect. Now the Dark Beasts won't be able to get into the Elf Woods anymore."

Fio didn't move a muscle. She felt like she'd been hit with dragon breath or something. After a long, uncomfortable period of silence, she spoke. "Um...Uncle Alan? I have a question."

"Yes?"

She had no idea how she was supposed to ask this. She struggled to put it into words. "Wh-where did you get the materials to build the bridges?" Anyone eavesdropping would get the impression that this wasn't the question she really wanted to ask.

"There are all kinds of stones on the ground, no?"

"Correct."

"There are even more of those beneath the surface."

"I see," Fio said.

"And that's that."

"Oh... What?" After a few seconds, Fio gave up. She smiled a smile that meant she had abandoned the very concept of understanding the present situation. A smile that screamed, *all's well that ends well.* Fio loved Alan, so she used that love to ignore the madness that had just unfolded. "Um, thank you so much! I can finally be at ease!"

"It's too early to give thanks. I gotta build your castle now."

"What?" Fio's smile froze in place.

"A trench and high walls aren't gonna keep out an army. A highly trained squad could easily get past this, so now I'm going to build you a castle guard."

Alan raised his shovel toward the heavens. It erupted with a blue aura, and when Alan pointed the shovel at a nearby empty space, the blue light coalesced, eventually taking the form of another, separate shovel. As the light faded, the new shovel began to move about of its own volition, walking on its metal blade.

Alan had created a Shovel Soldier, an autonomous being capable of digging up all sorts of things and places. It was also capable of combat. The Shovel Soldier came equipped with a Mini Wave Motion Shovel Blast. In long-range combat, it had the power of over ten average knights.

Alan made ninety-nine of them.

"Now if a human army tries to invade—Fio, what's wrong? You look a bit sick."

"No, I, um...I..." Fio looked up at the sky, her mind screaming at her. *What's happening? Am I the one who doesn't make sense here? I must be! This must be what common sense is for humans!* As it turned out, the well-endowed elf girl was extremely good at convincing herself that things were, in fact, totally fine. "S-so now the forest is safe, right?"

"No, not yet. The real fun starts now."

Fio froze up yet again.

"I haven't actually made the castle itself." He'd already built a trench, castle walls, and an army of soldiers that could rival a thousand men. Sure, the odds were in Fio's favor should an invading force of humans approach, but it still wasn't enough for Alan.

"Huh?! Um, if it can defend against an invading force, isn't that more than enough?"

"You're naive, Fio. Too naive. This isn't enough. Not by a long shot." Alan looked like a man possessed. "For example, what if a massive force of dragons came flying in?"

Several moments passed. "I would assume it to be the end of the world and give up," Fio answered with a smile that implied that she'd already given up in a number of ways.

"You can't give up hope so easily," Alan told her. "That sort of thing happened underground all the time."

"Um, but here on the surface, groups of dragons don't really attack on a regular basis."

"Is that so? Well, it never hurts to be prepared."

He then told Fio that massive numbers of elder dragons existed deep inside of Hell, in the dungeon known as the Dragon Nest. Alan had no trouble fighting them one on one, but against a whole army of them, he'd struggled.

That was when he'd invented the Attack Shovel Fortress. It was a powerful fortress capable of defending against the dragons' fire breath before shooting the creatures out of the sky.

"And that's why you have to be on guard against dragons," he finished. "Understand, Fio?"

"I understand." *That I don't understand a single thing that's happened here today,* she finished silently.

"Perfect. Watch from over there. This should take me about half an hour."

"I doubt I'll be able to see anything," Fio replied. Her uncle worked too fast for her eyes to keep up with.

Thus, Alan began constructing the fortress that would come to be known as the World Tree Castle. It was located in the center of the woods. In order for it to be capable of shooting an elder dragon out of the sky, the miner built it to be over nine hundred feet tall. At that point, it was basically a tower. The miner also made sure it was built out of adamantine. Not only could it withstand a Great Wyrm's breath, it also had auto-recovery abilities.

Alan thrust his shovel into various spots on the castle. By injecting these spots with his Shovel Power, he created auto-firing Anti-Air Shovel Cannons that would detect enemies and fire Mini Wave Motion blasts. He'd used these as his primary offensive force back during the Jewel War.

Finally, after half an hour of work, a majestic and beautiful castle stood before him. Alan stuck the blade of his shovel into the ground. "The elf castle is complete!" he declared with satisfaction.

The entirety of the Elf Woods was surrounded by a trench and the castle's walls. Should it be attacked, the Shovel Soldiers would respond in kind. Should an enemy approach from the sky, they'd be riddled with holes by the Shovel Cannons. Altogether, it was an invincible fortress that could withstand an apocalypse.

It was time to hold the completion ceremony. Alan would have Fio cut the tape, of course.

During this entire process, Fio had simply kept whispering "Shovels... Shovels..." to herself. From eradicating the Dark Beasts to putting the finishing touches on the castle, it had taken Alan only two short hours to build a castle as mighty as the legendary World Tree itself. According to the miner, this was all because of his Shovel Power. "What exactly is...a shovel?"

It was as though Fio was asking the universe itself. *What is a shovel?* It was a question that Alan had spent years upon years asking himself.

The shovel could fire a Wave Motion Shovel Blast. It could dig trenches, create soldiers, and build castles. None of it obeyed the laws of common sense. Alan used to think the same way during the first hundred years he'd studied the shovel, but now, he no longer questioned it. He could do nearly anything just by focusing his energy into his shovel.

If one were to ask Alan how that could be, he would have no answer. He just did it. He bypassed every scientific and magical rule of the world and came out the other side. A shovel, he'd decided, was the power to overcome the world itself.

⊢————▶

"...Anyway, so that's what went down. This is Fio, by the way." Alan introduced his niece. It was some time later after Alan had completed his construction project. He had gone back for Lithisia and Catria and brought them to the great hall of the World Tree Castle to meet the latest member of his family. He also took the opportunity to fill them in on what had transpired, nearly causing Catria to pass out.

"What did you *do*?" the knight wailed. She looked out at the castle wall at the edge of the Elf Woods from one of the windows. It was a glistening structure that stretched as far as the eye could see. She felt as though she was in the realm of the gods.

"No worries. I designed the wall so that light, rain, and wind could get through just fine. It'll have no effect on the natural order of the forest."

"Sir Miner's shovely wonderful concern for nature is truly shoveltastic!" The less said about Lithisia, however, the better.

"Let's make camp here for tonight," Alan suggested.

Fio had no problem with that. If anything, she felt that the castle belonged to Alan. The elf girl was gripping the miner's wrist as she glanced at Lithisia. This was her first time meeting a human other than Alan, and she was nervous. If the princess noticed, she didn't mention it.

"It's a pleasure to meet you, Lady Fioriel!" Lithisia said as she held up her dress and gracefully curtsied. "My name is Lithisia, and I am the crown princess of Rostir. It's an honor to make your acquaintance!"

"Aaah! You're a princess?!" Fio cried, waving her hands in a flustered fashion while her ample breasts jiggled about. She was clearly overwhelmed by Lithisia's royal aura, which was to be expected. Even Alan felt like the princess was hard to get close to...especially when she was going on and on about shovels.

Lithisia giggled as she watched Fio. "Don't be nervous. I hear you're a part of Sir Miner's family?"

"Oh, um, yeah, I suppose so..."

"She is," said the miner. "She's basically like my niece."

Fio made small embarrassed noises, which Lithisia promptly ignored.

"Then...that means you're my family, too!" the princess told the elf girl.

"Really? What kind of relationship do you have with Uncle Alan?" Fio asked.

Lithisia exuded the aura of a prim and proper princess as she gave an answer that was anything but. "Hee hee. Sir Miner and I..." She lowered her voice conspiratorially. "...are exclusively 'shoveling' together."

All the seriousness in the air crumbled into pieces. Fio blinked and looked at the miner. "Um...Uncle Alan?" she asked slowly.

"Sorry. I couldn't begin to tell you what she's going on about."

It was then that Lithisia gripped Fio's hand tightly. "Ah!" the elf girl cried, startled.

"But more importantly!" Lithisia shouted excitedly as her eyes sparkled. "Lady Fioriel, you must be one of the elves spoken of in the legends! Ever since I was a child, I've hoped to speak to an elf in person!" The princess was beaming as she continued. "Would you do me the honor of being my friend?"

Fio was so stunned that she nearly leapt away. "H-huh?! You want me to be your friend?! But you're a princess!"

"I just want to talk to you so very much!" Lithisia said. "About the elven legends, memories of your family, the legendary elven sweets, elven festivals, the elven capital and elven jewels... I just want to hear all about *you*!" Lithisia looked Fio straight in the eyes. "What do you say, Lady Fioriel?"

"Um..."

Lithisia's smile faded a little. "Do you not want to talk to me? I know I'm a bit of a naive princess, but I could tell you everything there is to know about Rostir. Um, um, the White Rose Capital, the Knights of the Seven Stars, the Rainbow Grasslands, Lugar's Ancient Artifact, and so much more! Lady Fioriel, please be my friend!" the princess begged once more before going silent, watching for the elf's reaction.

Fio considered the princess' proposal, despite her confused state. Of course she wanted to be friends with her.

F-friends with a real princess...

Fio was an elf, but she was also a young lady. There was so much that she wanted to ask the girl in front of her. Princess Lithisia, with her radiant smile and beautiful white dress, her golden blonde locks kept in perfect condition... Just what exactly did it take to become such a pure, beautiful princess? More importantly, why was she traveling with Uncle Alan?

Fio would get to talk with this princess as much as she wanted, and just thinking about it made her heart race. "A-am I dreaming?"

"Lady Fio?" Lithisia asked.

"I-I mean, the legendary Old Digger is my uncle, I get to meet a beautiful princess, and she even wants to be my friend..." Fio shook her head back and forth. "N-no matter how I look at it, I have to be dreaming."

Catria glared at Alan. What had he done to this poor girl?

"Don't give me that look," he told the knight. "All I did was build a castle."

"'All I did'? Really?" If this miner was left to his own devices, he'd probably save the world in two seconds and think nothing of it.

Alan tapped his shovel on the ground. "You're not dreaming, Fio."

The sound of splashing water found its way to Fio's ears. "Huh...?" When she turned around, the water in the cup sitting atop the table began to move. Soon, it took the form of a small, naked girl, who smiled at Fio.

"Dine?!" Fio gasped. It was her spirit friend, the very same one who had vanished after protecting Fio from the Dark Beasts.

"I noticed there was some water trapped inside the Beasts, so I used my shovel to collect it all," Alan explained.

Fio panicked and approached her old friend, picking up the cup that she was resting in. She could hear something inside.

"Fio, don't cry. Don't cry," came a small voice from the water. It was the same voice she had grown so used to hearing as she was growing up. Her best friend's kind voice. How could she not cry?

"Ah... Dine... Dine, I... I... Ahhhh..." The tears flowed. This was a future she had never even allowed herself to dream of. "Thank you so much, Uncle Alan... I..."

That was when she finally knew it was real.

$$\triangleright\!\!\!-\!\!\!-\!\!\!\rightarrow\!\!\blacksquare$$

Minutes later, Fio and Dine were drinking tea together with Lithisia. The elf was smiling brightly, listening to the princess' stories.

"...I guess the princess has more on her mind than just shovels."

"I guess so."

It didn't take long for Lithisia and Fio to become fast friends. Perhaps that shouldn't have been so surprising considering the former was a charismatic princess.

Alan looked at his niece. She had lived alone in the woods her entire life, so having a friend close to her age could only become a good thing. Alan was glad he introduced the two. *This'll be good for Fio.* Immediately after the thought crossed his mind...

"Lady Fio, let's chat all night! Especially about..." Lithisia's eyes lit up dangerously. "Shovels!"

Alan groaned inwardly.

▷━━━▶

That night, Fio appeared in Alan's bedroom. She was clad in elven attire, but something was off about her. She was crouched on the floor beside Alan's bed, her cheeks flushed. Perhaps more alarming was her ample bosom. It was as if she were positioned to deliberately draw attention to it.

Fio pressed her boobs together, making them appear even larger than they already were. Alan had never seen an elf as buxom as her before. "Um, please don't look at me... Er, I mean, please...look at me!"

Laid across the tops of Fio's firm breasts was Lithisia's red shovel.

The same shovel the princess had once used to try to seduce Alan.

Alan felt a horrible sense of déjà vu. It didn't take much for him to figure out from whom Fio had gotten this awful idea. The elf's legs were trembling, tears falling from her eyes. She was embarrassed, incapable of even looking Alan in the face.

This is madness.

Alan was filled with despair and a sense of emptiness. It was his fault that the elf had met the princess. That very well might have been the greatest mistake of his thousand-year-long life.

"Uncle, um, um, p-please—"

Alan cut her off. "I already know why you're doing this, so just calm down, Fio."

"No, I-I have to do this! I have to!"

"You really don't. In fact, you absolutely must not."

"I want to restore the elf village! I have to do this!" Fio was so nervous that she wasn't hearing Alan's words. "That's why... Uncle Alan, please take this naughty elf and...!" the elf cried as she drew his attention to the shovel atop her breasts. "Please 'shovel' with me!"

Alan buried his face in his hands and thought, *That princess is no shoveling good.*

INTERMISSION
Fioriel's Shovel of Happiness

THE MOONLIGHT SPILLED into Alan's room inside the World Tree Castle, illuminating both the white sheets covering his bed and the elf girl seated upon them.

Even in the dark, her shoulder-length golden blonde hair shone radiantly. Sitting atop her jiggling breasts was a small shovel. Regardless of whether Fio was moving or sitting still, the shovel was in no danger of falling off. Alan desperately wanted to tell her to remove it, but she vehemently refused.

"I'm so sorry, barging in during the night like this... Did I surprise you?" Fio asked.

"You did."

"I'm so, so sorry!" she apologized as she began to explain the events leading up to her actions. "After everything calmed down, Miss Lithisia and I talked about all manner of things..."

It was at that very moment that Alan vowed to never leave this pure young girl alone with the princess ever again.

"And then I realized s-something..." Fio turned away from Alan. "Even if the Elf Woods goes back to normal, I'm the only one who'll live h-here."

She wasn't wrong. Alan and Lithisia were on a journey, which meant that they couldn't stick around. Who would want to come back to such a sad place? "Hrm..." Alan said.

"But... But I want to bring back the town!"

"In other words...?"

"So... So... In order to do that, I..." Fio stopped speaking and turned her glistening eyes to Alan. "I have to do as much 'shoveling' as possible!"

The miner had been following her train of thought up until the very end, when she instantly became incomprehensible.

Alan wanted to hold his head in his hands. Lithisia had poisoned her mind. Of course, he was ultimately to blame for all of this. By introducing Fio to the princess, he was merely spreading the disease. He might have to quarantine her in the name of world peace at the rate things were going.

But Fio was the priority at the moment. While her words and actions—especially the Breast Shovel, as he'd begun internally calling it—were absurd, her actual goal was the real deal.

Fio was family. He had to save her from Lithisia's influence. Alan decided to just ask her, point-blank, "Fio, when you say 'shoveling', what exactly do you mean?"

Lithisia had been increasing the amount of meanings the word "shovel" and its permutations could have at an alarming rate. At some point, she would probably replace an entire dictionary's worth of words with "shovel." This meant that Alan had to figure out the context in this particular sentence.

"What?! Y-you want me to explain that?! To you?!" Fio panicked, but the shovel on her breasts didn't budge. "Um, well, it's basically the creation of life."

"Be more specific."

"B-but Lithisia told me that you'd understand if I said 'shoveling'!"

"As if. Also, don't ever trust anything she says. Ever."

"Wh-wh-what? You want me to be even more specific?!" She squirmed, her bountiful breasts swaying back and forth. Fio put both hands on her burning hot cheeks. "Um, well, you touch like this..." Fio's beautiful white hands began to move. "And, um, gently caress... And then finally..." She muttered the rest under her breath.

"Fio, I can't hear you."

"I said, you, um, aaah..." Fio finally blurted it out. "Love! You give love shape! In the nude!"

"'Give love shape in the nude'...?" Alan was still puzzled.

"P-please don't make me explain anymore! I beg of you!"

Alan thought to himself. She could mean one of two things. The first, of course, was the romantic activity that two lovers performed together. *There's no way she means that,* he thought. There was simply no way that anyone would ever choose someone like him—a miner who could do naught but dig up jewels—as a lover. Which meant...

"I see. I understand now."

"You do?!"

"Yes. It's the whole kneading thing, right?"

"E-excuse me?!" Fio held her breasts tightly. "I...I suppose you could say that, yes!"

Alan nodded. He was right on the mark. The "shoveling" that Fio was referring to was...

Sculpting.

▷━━━▶

The elf village was once renowned as a city dedicated to fine arts. When Alan visited some four hundred years ago, there was a series of statues in the center of the village.

The residents would pay tribute to them during festivals. If Fio was to revive the village, she would absolutely need statues. Alan was certain of this.

Unfortunately, he was a stubborn man when it came to his beliefs. He was actually fairly similar to Lithisia in that sense. He twisted Fio's words around in his head to match his theory.

The "creation of life" referred to a hero's life, which would be captured in the finished statue. To "gently caress" referred to the process of preparing clay. Finally, to "give love shape in the nude" meant sculpting a nude statue.

Alan had always thought that the nude statues the elves made were among the most beautiful sculptures in the world.

I must be right. Fio wants me to make one of those for her.

Which meant that her whole Breast Shovel thing was her own attempt at art, even if it was excessively provocative.

"But Fio, I'm not what you'd call a pro. Are you sure you're okay with me?"

Fio's cheeks turned pink as she looked down, her hands pressed against her breasts as tears dripped from her eyes. "I...um, I know my body is weird..." Her breasts trembled. It was indeed weird how large they were. "You're the only one who pays any attention to me, Uncle Alan."

"No, hold on. Your body has nothing to do with it." By "it," Alan of course meant "art." "What's important is your heart."

Fio looked up with a smile. Thanks to Alan leaving out the important details, Fio had completely misunderstood him. "Uncle Alan, you're so kind... That's why I..." She took a deep breath and looked him straight in the eyes. "No matter how embarrassing it is...and it's really, really embarrassing..." Fio took a deep breath. Alan was her hero. She could think of no better person to ask. She knelt on the floor, her breasts jiggling, and cried, "I want you to 'shovel' with me!"

Alan could do nothing but nod his head. Their single shot at undoing this awful misunderstanding was lost for all of eternity. "Got it. I'll do my best."

Fio responded with a shy smile.

"I may not be a professional, but I do know what to do."

"Um..." Fio raised her hand. "I was just wondering... Can one really be a professional at this kind of thing?"

"Of course," Alan said. "Pasarunak was a pro, actually."

Fio nearly jumped up in surprise. "The elder was a pro?!"

"You didn't know? He probably had something like a thousand under his belt."

"One thousand people?! I-I had no idea he was like that!"

"Mmm-hmm. I've even watched him doing it." Sculpting, of course. "The way he moved his hands was something else."

"Something else?! Aaaaaaahhh!" And just like that, Fio's impressions of her ancestor had shifted dramatically. Her entire face was bright red. *What could he mean by "something else"?!* She was tremendously interested, but she didn't dare ask.

"You should study up as well, Fio. You're related to him. I'm sure you have the same latent abilities."

"Oh my gosh..." Fio grabbed both of her cheeks with her hands. She shyly turned away from Alan. "Would... you be happy if I got good at it, Uncle Alan?"

"Hm? Of course I would." With enough practice, Alan felt his niece would be an excellent sculptor.

"Y-you would...? I see... Oh gosh..." Fio looked at her hands through her tear-filled eyes. Eventually, she used one of those hands to hide her face. "A-all right. I'm going to do my best to get good!"

"I know you can do it," Alan encouraged her. "Good luck!"

Fio blushed. "Th-thank you!"

Misunderstandings like this were seemingly never-ending.

"Now then, how about we get going? Let's start with the basics."

"I-I'm in your hands!" Fio said excitedly.

And so Alan began to work. Using his shovel, he collected enough clay to sculpt a single statue. The key to producing high-quality clay was to knead it thoroughly. He stuck his shovel into the stuff and began to mix it together roughly at first, then more gently. After he'd gotten it to a certain level of softness, he used his hands to stir the clay.

"H-huh...?" Fio watched him work with a puzzled expression on her face. "I-Is this really practice...?"

"Of course," he replied. Sculpting was the real deal. It required a lot of prep work. "Everything begins with practice," Alan said as he kneaded the clay thoroughly. Fio once again held her arms to her breasts tightly.

Alan gently rubbed the clay over and over again.

"You do it this gently...?"

"It's just like I said, Fio. You gotta put lots of love into it."

"Love..." she repeated softly.

Alan picked up some clay and began to knead it with his hands. For some reason, Fio reacted to each motion, her breasts bouncing about. Even worse was that she was sitting on the floor in a super short skirt, holding her knees to her chest. Alan could just barely see a hint of white beneath the hem. Her closed thighs were something to behold.

Alan had no place to look at his niece safely. *I have to focus,* he admonished himself. He couldn't think of the girl like this. Not as her uncle. He chased off the lewd thoughts and concentrated on the clay, paying no mind to Fioriel's breathy comments as she watched him work.

"Oh my gosh... You're so gentle... Aaaah!" With every motion the miner made, Fio's breasts bounced about. "If you keep going like that, I'll, I'll...!" The elf girl cried out joyously, but Alan continued to knead. "Ah, if you grip them that roughly, I..."

Alan kneaded the clay beneath the moonlight while the elf girl thrashed about. If someone else were to see the two of them, they would've undoubtedly asked themselves, *What in blue blazes are they doing?!*

▷━━━━━▶

Two hours had gone by since practice began. "That's step one done," Alan finally said.

"Haaah, haaah...." Fio was drenched in sweat as she caught her breath. Her clothes were almost entirely see-through at this point, showing the color of her skin, as well as the pink peaks on each breast. Her milky white thighs peeped from beneath her skirt.

"Whoa, Fio! Are you okay?!"

"Aaah, I…I'm okay… Haaah, haaah…."

Alan drew close, and Fio rested up against him. Her hair smelled wonderful, and her skin was springy and soft to the touch. Alan was assaulted by all kinds of wonderful sensations.

"I-I'm sorry," she apologized. "I know we should be practicing 'shoveling,' but…"

"No, I'm glad you're taking things so seriously. So, what do you think?" he asked. He definitely wanted to know her thoughts on the art of sculpting.

For a time, Fio simply grasped the cuff of Alan's shirt sleeve. "I could… I could feel the love." The elf girl's eyes were basically spinning in circles. She must've really exhausted herself.

"Are you all right?" he asked, concerned. "You should get some rest."

Fio nodded her head and leaned closer against him. Alan felt bad about forcing her to move from her spot, so he simply caressed her beautiful blonde hair.

"Ah, that feels so good…" the elf girl sighed.

"Does it? Then I'll keep going." Alan continued to caress her hair gently, almost as if he were singing her a lullaby.

"I'm…shovely happy…" Fio began to whisper in her sleep, her breasts pressed up against Alan's arm.

Wait, do I have to stay like this all night?

Fio's mighty bosom continued to press against Alan's arm as she breathed in and out. Unfortunately for Alan, this trial would last all the way until sunrise.

⊳━━━➤

The next day...

"Lithisia, you filled Fio's head with all kinds of shovel weirdness, didn't you?"

The princess, Catria, and Alan faced the morning with cups of black tea in hand. Needless to say, the topic of conversation was the way Fio acted the night before.

"Sir Miner, the shovel is required religious learning for all of humanity," she replied. Alan shook his head. If that was the case, Rostir's future was in great danger. "By the way, um, how was Fio?" Lithisia asked, clearly curious about his answer. He noticed that she'd stopped referring to the elf as "Lady Fio."

"She took things very seriously. She told me something about how she could feel the love."

"Feel...the love?!" Flustered, Lithisia began wringing her hands. "Um, I'm sorry. I guess I'm a little jealous."

"Why? You're the one who set her on the path, no?"

"Sir Miner, you're too great for me, a simple princess, to monopolize..."

Alan scoffed at that. "Surely you jest. I'm not that big a deal."

"Sir Miner." Lithisia's expression was serious. "Anyone who visits this forest will immediately understand just how incredible a person you are." She pointedly looked out the window of the elf castle. A massive trench surrounding the entirety of the forest, an adamantine wall stretching as far as the eye could see, the massive World Tree Castle itself... All of it had taken Alan only two hours to construct.

He'd made a castle capable of piercing the heavens like it was no big deal. Creation on that level was the territory of the gods.

"Sir Miner, one day you will be spoken of in legend." Lithisia tried to hide the melancholy in her voice. It was a feeling that didn't suit her. "That's why I'm... Well, I'm happy just to be by your side... Aaah!"

Lithisia let out a startled cry as Alan ruffled her golden hair. He couldn't stand seeing her looking so sad. He almost preferred her when she was going on and on about shovels. "Lithisia, I'm just a miner. There's no reason to worship me like some kind of god. You and I are just regular old humans."

The princess stared at Alan's face for a time before the tears started coming. She eventually nodded. "I'm...I'm shovely happy..." Lithisia whispered the same thing Fio had the previous night. "But I'm still going to worship you. I've already decided that our religion's object of worship will be a golden shovel."

"*Please* don't go deciding things like that."

"Oh, and I've chosen Catria as the captain of the Holy Shovel Knights. Talk about a promotion, right?"

"I'd like to turn in my notice of resignation," Catria replied dryly.

"Nope! Not allowed."

"...Whatever," Alan surrendered. "Let's get ready to go."

According to what Fio had told him, the Ancient Castle of Riften had become a nest for the undead. The entire building was already covered in a creepy yellow aura, skeletons and ghosts coming and going in and out of its doors and windows. It was very likely that the inside of the building was now a dungeon.

A dungeon was a miner's true calling. He turned to the knight. "Catria, what's the most important thing one must remember about a dungeon?"

"Easy. That one must battle with great courage."

"Wrong."

Catria blinked. "Huh?"

"The key point in conquering any dungeon is..." Alan paused dramatically. A blue aura of energy began to emanate from behind him, signaling his readiness. "Safety first!" he proclaimed.

Thus began the safest dungeon run in the history of the continent.

PART 9
The Miner and His "Safety First" Dungeon Run

THE GROUP HAD left a tearful Fioriel behind at her home before setting out for the Ancient Castle of Riften. The elf girl made them promise to swing by on the way back. Several hours later, the party cleared the forest and were met with a wide-open plain.

"Sir Miner! This is Riften's famous Galessa Shovel!" Lithisia exclaimed.

"Your Royal Highness, I think you mean the Galessa Steppe," Catria corrected her.

"In honor of Sir Miner's elf castle, I took the liberty of renaming it."

"Please don't."

"Too late!" She stuck her tongue out at the knight. Catria didn't bother with a response. Lithisia was too far gone.

Alan was more than happy to leave arguing with the princess to Catria. He looked toward the ancient castle that sat atop a small hill on the plains.

The castle wall had broken down, all manner of plants growing over the surface. It was still in the distance, but even from where he was, Alan could see the yellow aura surrounding it. That aura signified the presence of the undead. Once, the castle had been the home of a huge royal family. Now, it was nothing more than a nest for evil.

"Somewhere beneath that castle is the Blue Orb," Lithisia said. "I bet Sir Miner could grab it in two seconds with his shovel!"

"Your Royal Highness, surely you jest. That's a castle of horrors. Even Sir Alan couldn't possibly..." Catria trailed off, realizing her argument didn't stand up to the miracles she'd already seen.

"Tell that to the World Tree Castle," Lithisia retorted. "The captain of the Holy Shovel Knights needs to properly understand the true power of the shovel."

A bead of sweat made its way down Catria's forehead. It was true. This man might actually be able to do what the princess proposed. "W-well, Sir Alan? Can you get the orb?"

Alan thought for a moment. "I can."

It was that simple.

"I knew you could do it, Sir Miner! I shovely believed!" Lithisia exclaimed.

"You can...?" Catria sighed in resignation. Of course he could do it. He could seemingly do anything.

"Wait, wait, Catria. I *can* do it, but I didn't say I *would*."

"Huh?" Lithisia and Catria simultaneously tilted their heads. "What's that supposed to mean, Sir Alan?" the knight asked.

"For example, let's say I used my Shovel Wave Motion Shovel Blast to blow away the entire castle."

"Your example is absurd, but go on."

"What if there happened to be a powerful monster lurking within that had a reflection barrier?"

Seconds passed in silence. "...Are there monsters capable of doing that?" Catria asked.

"Beneath the surface, there are. There was one beneath the mountain I lived on." It was the single most powerful creature he had met in his thousand years of life.

Where the 6,666th layer of the jewel mountain connected with the Alter Genesis of Amber was a territory controlled by the Demogorgon, the King of Hell. It was a place of molten rivers and ashen skies, of blue and white lightning, and of death. It was in this hell that Alan suddenly found himself under assault by a rocky mountain.

Except it hadn't been a mountain. It was the massive body of the Demogorgon.

That said, Alan was an experienced miner. He immediately understood the situation he was in and fired off the Wave Motion Shovel Blast without a second thought.

KAAAAAA-BOOOOOOOOOOM.

"What?!"

The Demogorgon had reflected Alan's beam in a silver flash. Actually, it was more like the beam had been moving in reverse. It should've been impossible for most magics to have any sort of effect on the Wave Motion Shovel Blast, and yet, the Demogorgon had reflected it. Alan would later find out that the Demogorgon had rewritten the laws of the world to reverse the beam's vector.

The miner discovered something important that day. He found out that deep below the surface lived creatures able to freely rewrite the laws of the world.

It had been a fierce battle. In the end, it was a blast from his Wave Motion Shovel Blast at point-blank range that defeated the creature. Despite coming out of the battle victorious, Alan had prepared himself for death. That was how serious things had gotten. He would not presume that there were no such creatures on the surface of the planet.

"And that's why safety is the number one priority when it comes to dungeon runs," he finished.

"Whoa, wait, wait, wait!" Catria immediately cut in. "The Demogorgon is a creature that appears in creation myths! It's the Great Demon whose power is said to rival that of even the Dark Lord!"

"So that was the Great Demon? Hrm. No wonder it was so powerful."

Catria furiously shook her head. "No, no, no, no, absolutely not! This is impossible! Use common sense!"

"Wow, so Sir Miner is already a legend," Lithisia sighed. "Ah, how shovelful!"

"Either way, safety is our first priority. This is for your training too, Catria."

"Wait, me?" Catria asked.

"You want to be strong like me, right?"

"I...well..."

"That's what you said when we first met, was it not?"

"I mean, yes, but..." Catria had to admit he had a point, but she'd only said that because she'd mistaken him for a swordsman.

Alan nodded. "The basics are generally the same between swords and shovels. I'll teach you what you need to know as we progress through the dungeon."

"B-but I really don't need you to teach me..." Catria was not about to become some sort of weird shovel devotee like the princess. What would the other knights think?

"You'll get stronger," Alan pointed out. "Trust me. I'm the number one miner on this planet. I can tell you've got talent. Let me mine it out of you."

"Urrgh…" Catria groaned. The miner's attempts at baiting her were working like a charm. It was like he was dangling a large diamond in front of her. *He thinks I have talent,* she thought. How could she not be happy that the strongest man in the world felt that way about her? "…I-If it doesn't work out, I'm quitting, got it?"

"Of course."

Catria couldn't help but let a small smile slip onto her face.

▷━━━━━▶

First on the list of objectives was info collection. Alan created some Shovel Soldiers and had them dig into the dungeon, checking for things like monsters, traps, and routes. Once the information had made its way back to the miner, he projected a Dungeon Run Guide onto the blade of his shovel. The metal was polished to a mirror-like sheen, displaying everything they would need to know about the dungeon.

"Wait…" Catria apparently had questions. "What the hell just happened?! How do you have a perfect map already?!"

"Dungeon runs are war."

"War?!"

"Exactly. And in war, information is the difference between life and death."

As he taught Catria the ropes, Alan looked over the info on his shovel. Generally speaking, they were looking at a whole lot of undead enemies. Catria could take care of them on her own with a little help from Alan, but he refused to take the risk. It was possible that a God-class creature could be feeding him false info. After all, "safety first" was the name of the game.

"All right," Alan said. "Our first priority is to completely isolate the dungeon from the outside world."

"What do you mean?" Catria asked.

"Catria, when it comes to war, enemy backup is the scariest thing of all."

"What's your point?"

"We're going to put up a barrier so that even if a giant squad of dragons came as backup, we'd be fine."

Catria looked up at the sky. It was perfectly clear; excellent weather for kite flying. There was no way a group of dragons could ambush them from this beautiful sky. "What is your deal with dragons?" she asked. "Do you have some kind of dragon-related trauma or something...?"

"Yes," he replied matter-of-factly.

"...Oh."

Once when Alan was mining for jewels, he was attacked by a group of dragons that had been summoned out of nowhere. He'd barely escaped with his life. So in the spirit of "safety first," Alan felt they required a countermeasure against wandering dragons.

Alan drew up a shovel circle (the shovel equivalent of a magic circle, shaped like a shovel) with his shovel and booted up the barrier. Unlike the barrier he'd created for the Elf Woods, this one didn't need to be permanent. As a result, it only took him twenty seconds to surround the entirety of the ancient castle. With that, they'd no longer have to be concerned about outside interference.

"Whoa..." Catria stared at the castle with dead eyes.

The gigantic barrier surrounding the castle let off a bizarre humming noise. Even if one were to gather all of the continent's mages together in one place and conducted a hundred-year casting ritual, they'd be unable to create a barrier this large.

What the hell is this?!

"A shovel barrier... It's shovely cool!"

Lithisia's comments only served to further confuse the knight. *Please, shut up.* "Argh! A-Alan, let's hurry up and start the dungeon run!"

"Absolutely not. I'm only just getting started making things safe."

"Making things safe?"

"Correct. I'm going to do a good old dungeon reform."

The dungeon in question was three floors deep and four floors tall, but it was filled with narrow passageways and all kinds of death traps. These were the things that Alan would have to take care of. He'd create one easy-to-navigate passageway and bury all the traps with his shovel.

But even then, there was the possibility of unseen enemies lurking in the shadows, the kinds that could stay off the grid. Alan dug a warp hole into the passageway, just in case they had to make an emergency exit.

"Never forget. Making things safe is the key to a successful dungeon run."

Construction wrapped up in three minutes flat. Catria simply looked at the map of the reformed dungeon with an empty expression on her face.

"What's wrong, Catria? Is there something you're still worried about?"

"I... Ever consider countermeasures for if a meteor fell on your head?"

Catria was coming up against the limits of her patience.

"A meteor, eh? I hadn't thought of that."

"..."

"It's true, though. The surface is at risk of falling meteors. Catria, put this on." Alan plopped a helmet on her head with a sticker reading "Safety First!" plastered on it. It covered up her beautiful red ponytail, but nobody was thinking about that at the moment.

Catria was dead. Well, she was alive, but psychologically, she was dead. Catria of the Dead.

"Perfect. Time to head in!"

The front gate of the castle was old and covered in dangerous thorns, so Alan got rid of it. He replaced it with a cream-colored door that wouldn't have been out of place on a palace. Catria opened it, her eyes still dead. A single skeleton came running at her, and the knight instinctively took a combat stance.

It was then that she noticed the ground was shockingly easy to move across. In fact, it was waxed like a gymnasium.

"..."

Catria defeated the skeleton with three strikes, and watched it fall to pieces on the floor.

"...Alan."

"Yes?"

Catria seemed to want to say something, but kept stopping herself beforehand. She repeated this a handful of times before eventually deciding she didn't care anymore. "Alan... What exactly is a dungeon run?"

"War."

"War, eh? I get it now. It's war. Hahaha..." Catria dropped her sword to the ground and looked up. The miner said he would teach her how to mine, but all she had learned was one simple fact. "I never realized that war was so empty..."

And thus did Catria grow as a knight.

"By the way, Sir Miner. Could you teach Catria how to make dungeons safe?"

"Wha?"

"It'd take about two years, by my estimations."

"I don't mind. She's the captain of the Holy Shovel Knights. She's what everyone will aspire to."

"Whoa, hold on, Your Royal Highness!"

"Got it. First let me prepare a shovel just for her."

"Stoooooooooop"

Catria's trials and tribulations had only just begun.

In the end, Catria was unable to push back against her princess' wishes, and was ultimately forced to shoulder a shovel.

"This is just a tool! A tool for exploring dungeons! That's it! Don't worry!" Her eyes were filled with tears as she repeated these words to herself.

The trio managed to safely make their way through the dungeon, eventually arriving at the deepest area of the castle. Despite the condition of the building itself, the treasure room was still as beautiful as ever. In the center was a pedestal, the Blue Orb shining radiantly atop it.

The entire room was illuminated by its divine blue light. It was almost as if its radiance was cleansing their very souls.

"Amazing... This is the orb spoken of in Rostir legend..." Catria had recovered from her zombie-like state just in time to express how moved she was by the orb in question. "Yeah! This is it! This is the kind of treasure hunting that gets the soul fired up!"

"Sir Miner, why is this room shovely clean and well-maintained?" Lithisia asked.

"When I made the map, I had my shovel soldiers clean the place up."

Smash. That was the sound of Catria slamming her head against one of the nearby pillars. "Why didn't you just have one of them grab the orb?!"

"Madness. They had one objective: safety first."

"Shoveling shovelberries (TL: that's our Sir Miner for you)!" Catria was at her wit's end. At this point, nobody outside of Lithisia could be bothered to figure out what she was actually saying. "What in the bloody world is wrong with you and that shovel of yours?!"

"Hrm. Behind you."

"Eh?"

The light blue aura surrounding the orb began to take the shape of a human. A young girl, in fact. Her entire body was transparent, and she had not an ounce of clothing on her. Her long, silver hair made her look like some kind of deity. Slotted into her forehead was a jewel that glowed a creepy black light.

The see-through girl floated in the air, eventually opening her eyes.

"Wha...? Is this the spirit that dwelled within the orb?"

"No, not quite."

Alan gripped his shovel.

The girl with the silver hair stared down at Alan and the others, then grinned. "Hee hee, puny humans. Fair sacrifices, welcome to my abode." As she spoke, her body began to glow a yellow aura, the very same one unique to the undead.

Catria immediately gripped her sword, not her shovel. "Dammit! This thing is the ruler of the castle!"

"I quite like smart humans. You shall become my kin!"

She emitted a pitch-black aura from the jewel on her forehead. Its power was incredible. Catria was at a loss for words. As a knight, she'd participated in numerous monster hunts, but she'd never seen a creature as strong as this.

"Urgh...!"

The pitch-black aura began to coil itself around Catria's body, but then, all of a sudden...

KA-CHOOOOM!

"Nngyaaa?!"

Catria's shovel exploded with bright light that snaked forward and eliminated the dark aura. The naked girl fell face first onto the floor. "Wh-what was that light?!" she howled, holding her head in pain.

"...What just happened?" Catria whispered to herself.

"The power of the shovel."

"Why does it always have to be a shovel thing with you?"

"No, seriously. It was the power of the 'Holy Knight Shovel' I gave you."

Catria cast her gaze to the silver shovel on her back. It was glowing as radiantly as the sun itself.

"Holy Knights have holy powers, do they not? When I gave you the shovel, I infused it with Divine Shovel Power."

"Sir Miner's Divine Shovel! That would surprise even the Holy Angel of Shovels!"

"No such angel exists."

"Then I'll make one later!"

Catria looked at the silver-haired undead girl cradling her head on the floor. When she aimed the shovel on her back in her direction...

"N-no! Stop!" the girl screamed.

Catria immediately felt bad for the undead girl. *Ah... This girl is just another victim.*

"Grr... H-how dware you do this to mwee! You insolent pest!" The undead girl rose to her feet while glaring at Catria. She was already fumbling her words, making her look like just an ordinary young girl. "D-don't look at me with those sympathetic eyes! I, the immortal Queen Alice Veknarl, will show you the true meaning of fear!"

A rumbling noise surrounded them. The castle began to shake like it was being struck by an earthquake, but this was no natural calamity—it was the sound of countless monsters racing across the ground.

Alice vanished. She'd probably fled the castle.

"An army, eh? Looks like it's my turn."

"Isn't it always?"

"It's not my fault that the shovel is useful in all situations. More importantly, let me teach you something, Catria."

"What?"

"The shovel is the most powerful weapon of all." Alan pointed his shovel directly at her eyes and firmly stated. "Especially on the battlefield."

A few seconds later, Catria looked up toward the heavens. How many times had she asked herself this, today alone?

What the heck is a shovel?

PART 10

The Princess Shovels the Immortal Alice

THE WAR had begun.

As soon as they exited the ancient castle, Alice was waiting for them outside with an army. The once empty Galessa Shovel (renamed by Lithisia) was now the stage for two forces standing off against one another: Alan's Holy Shovel Knights (named by Lithisia) and Alice's army of 10,000 undead.

"Can't we do something about our name and this flag...?" Catria was sadly holding a flag with a doodle of a shovel on it.

"Absolutely not. We must show these nonhumans how great the shovel is!"

"At this point, I'm starting to think that you're the real nonhuman," the knight replied, no longer capable of mincing words.

"What? But I... Compared to Sir Miner, I still have shovely long to go."

"Why are you getting all bashful? Argh, whatever. It's true that Alan is inhuman." Catria looked behind her.

There was nothing, and that in and of itself was bizarre. The massive ancient castle that she had only just finished exploring was nowhere to be found. As for why that was the case, well... Alan had dismantled it as soon as they exited in search of Alice.

In two seconds.

"Now that we have the orb, there's no point leaving this thing up if it's just going to serve as a den for the undead."

And so Alan crushed the castle like it was a nest for ants. Apparently, Alice didn't even notice the deconstruction as it happened.

Catria felt bad for her. "But Alan, wouldn't it be better to fight an army like this in tighter quarters?" In a wide-open space like this, the army with the greater numbers would have the advantage. They should've stayed in the castle. Considering Alan was always going on about "safety first," this felt like an odd choice.

"Hrm, you're right, but I wouldn't be able to inhume them."

"Inhume?"

"Yeah. In order to prevent them from coming back to life, we should bury them."

"Oh, right."

"So if we face them out in the field, we won't have to worry about where to dig graves."

"Yeah... Wait, what?" After thinking on Alan's words for a moment, Catria finally realized what he was getting at. "I really, really feel bad for that Alice girl..."

"You're all shoveled and ready to go!" *Munch, munch.* Lithisia was seated on the ground eating some elf snacks that Fio made.

"I'm shocked you have an appetite, given how it reeks of undead right now..."

"I plugged my nose with shovel-shaped tissues, so it's no problem at all."

No problem, except for the problem with her head.

"Would you like some, Catria? I still have some shovel-shaped ones."

"I'd prefer to stay human, thanks."

"You bastards! Stop stuffing your faces! Are you ready?!" Alice screamed. She sat haughtily in a portable shrine made from bones in the center of her army. For whatever reason, she was waiting to attack. She must've been confused by all the shovel nonsense.

"Shall we begin then?" Alan said.

"What's with that shovel of yours? What are you, some sort of clown? Bwahahaha!" Alice laughed. Her undead army, the Neo Riften Guard, was the strongest military force on the surface of the planet. There was no way she would lose to three humans. "Kill them all!"

And just like that, the shovel descended upon the battlefield.

The droves of undead shone like the surface of a river bathed in light. It was, in fact, the light reflected as Alan chopped off their heads, made graves, buried them in said graves, then hardened the ground with his shovel and built headstones.

"Woooow! You're the best, Sir Miner!"

Lithisia cheered for Alan as he built 10,000 graves. All Catria was able to catch with her eyes was a storm of light on the battlefield. The miner's "Light Speed Shoveling" was impossible to see with human eyes.

"The Last Shovel."

Alan stabbed his tool into the dirt. He was all done burying his enemies.

"I... What." Catria looked at the battlefield. "He made a graveyard."

There were in fact 10,000 headstones standing side by side. The stones themselves were sparklingly new, and each one read, "Here sleeps a nameless hero of Riften."

They even had flowers placed at their bases. In the center of the graveyard was a tower with a bell. The nail in the coffin (hah) was the requiem echoing throughout the area.

Its source? Alan's shovel, of course.

"..."

The requiem was enough to push Catria to her tipping point. Again.

"Make a few adjustments and a shovel can be a great musical instrument. The shovel head kinda resembles a guitar pick already, right?"

Right?! Are you kidding me?!

"My only regret is that I had to bury these fine folks without knowing their names."

WHO CARES?!

"Ah, Sir Miner! I would love if, when the time comes, you made my grave for me!"

"I have a headache..."

"Hrm? Are you okay? Want me to use my Shovel Healing on you?"

"Hell no! That'd just make things worse!"

"GAAAAAAAAAAAAHHHHHHHHHHHH?!"

It was then that they heard a cry coming from Queen Alice. "Why?! Why has my powerful army been turned into a graveyard?! What happened?!"

"The power of the shovel happened."

"What the heck does that mean?! What exactly is that thing?!"

Catria had asked the same question many times. She got the feeling that Alice would make for a wonderful friend had they met under better circumstances.

"Alan, what should we do with her?"

"She might have info about the other orbs. Let's capture her for now."

A second later, Alice was nude and tied up on the ground thanks to Alan's rope (???) shovel.

"What the hell?!"

"Alan, could you maybe take things a little more slowly? This is too much for me."

"I'll keep that in mind."

The young girl was tied up and completely in the buff, her silver hair resting on the ground. Alan's eyes were drawn to her barely developed chest. Though she was the queen of the undead, the miner felt somewhat guilty.

"Why?! How?! How could one with an astral body be tied up like this?!"

"The power of the shovel."

"Madness! As if a base tool like a shovel could ever have any kind of effect on an astral body!"

"A base...tool?" Lithisia responded to Alice.

Catria felt a chill run down her spine. Lithisia was smiling, but her eyes were not. For some reason, behind the princess was a shovel-shaped aura. She was actually terrifying.

"Sir Miner, could you leave her to me?"

What was she planning to do? Alan didn't dare ask, as it was all too clear that she was planning on "shoveling" the undead queen.

"Gaaah! S-stop it! Stop this at o-once!!!"

Alice cried out and squirmed, still tied up.

"Hee hee hee. Come on now, Lady Alice. This is just a 'base tool', right?"

"Stop! Don't come any closer! P-please! Just s-stop... Aaaaah!!"

"I will not stop."

With each adjustment Lithisia made to the shovel, Alice's body bent and contorted. For some reason, black sweat was pouring from the jewel in her forehead, as if it were screaming for Lithisia to stop as well.

"What exactly am I looking at?"

"Don't ask me."

Lord knows that if they asked Lithisia, she'd just answer with "shoveling" or something similar.

In any case, if one were to describe what they were watching unfold, it would be as such: Lithisia was running the tip of her red shovel across the bottoms of a young, naked, silver-haired girl's feet. Apparently the tool was extremely effective against the girl's astral body.

Tickle, tickle.

"F-for the love of! Please, stop! I can't take any... Hah hah hah!"

"Not yet! Let's shovel some more!"

"Aha! Hahahaha, nooooooooooooo!" The naked girl's nose was running, she had tears in her eyes, and she was drooling. What a mess.

"I never considered using a shovel for interrogation."

"Forget everything you're seeing! You can never use this against a human, ever!"

"Tell that to Lithisia."

Five minutes later, the young girl was on her knees apologizing, covered in tears and sweat and drool.

"I'm so so so so so so sorry, please forgive me! I'll tell you everything I know! Just no more of that infernal shovel, please!"

"Infernal...?"

"EEK! I-I mean that that the shovel is shovely shovel-tastically shoveltronically awesome!"

Alice was already a slave to Lithisia's will.

The princess wiped the sweat from her forehead and drew close to Alan. "Sir Miner! I put everything you taught me to good use!"

"Don't ever do that again." *What have I turned this princess into?*

But right now, Alice was priority number one.

"Now then... Who are you, exactly?"

Alice trembled in response to his question, but as soon as she looked at Lithisia's shovel, she began to shake even more violently. "I'm... I'm Riften's last queen."

Not that it matters once a shovel gets involved, Catria thought to herself.

PART 11
The Miner Becomes Alice's Hero

THE SELF-PROCLAIMED QUEEN of the undead, unable to withstand the intense shovel interrogation, began to tell Alan and his party about the circumstances that led her down this path.

"I died once... And was brought back to life.

Riften was destroyed in the great war 300 years ago, when Alice was the princess of the kingdom. The defeated royal family was murdered in its entirety. The king at the time, Alice's father, used "Veknar's Crown," one of Riften's royal treasures, in a last-ditch effort to save his daughter. It was said that the human who donned the crown would be able to return from the dead.

"I've heard of it before..."

"You know about it, Alan?"

"Layer #451 of the mountain was connected to the 'Shrine of Veknar,' where they worshipped the guy. His followers ended up summoning this monstrous version of him that I had to fight. The thing had a death ray and everything. It was super powerful. If I didn't have an anti-death attribute on my shovel, things would've been bad."

"Yeah, real bad (like your very existence)."

"Wow! You can even overcome death with your shovel!"

"No, I can't. I just managed not to die is all."

"Feel free to die when you want to. Anyway, let's just hurry up and get the rest of her story."

"O-okay... When I revived, my country was no more."

Alice had awoken in the family grave beneath the once proud castle. The building itself was falling apart. Tens of years had passed since Alice died, and the citizens of Riften had long since fled, leaving the territory to become home to all manner of monsters. That was when Alice decided to make citizens of her own.

She couldn't explain why or how she knew how to do this, but she did. The wisdom of necromancy came flooding into her from the crown on her head.

"Huh, so that thing is filled with Veknar's knowledge?"

"Precisely." It wasn't rare for Artifacts to grant their holders some kind of knowledge.

"On that day, I began to call myself Alice Veknarl. That's what my heart told me I was. It means 'successor of Veknar.'"

Lithisia nodded, struck by a revelation. "Sir Miner! Could we not make a Shovel Crown capable of passing on shovel knowledge?!"

"It already exists. The helmet I gave Catria has that kind of effect."

"Wha?!"

Catria immediately ripped off the safety first helmet on her head. How could she have been so foolish as to wear this brainwashing device without question?!

"Fear not. All it does is make sure you prioritize safety first."

"'Fear not', my ass! I'm not wearing anything you give me ever again!"

"Aw, c'mon. Don't be like that!" Lithisia added.

"Y-your Royal Highness! Let's hurry up and get the rest of Alice's story!"

"I suppose you're right. Lady Alice, look! A brand-new shovel."

"Eeek! Don't wave that thing around in front of me!"

Alice nervously continued her tale.

"B-but the citizens I made were all soulless corpses..."

Braindead skeletons and zombies. Low-tier liches.

That was the limit of Alice's abilities. And so, Alice sat on the throne of a castle filled with the shambling undead. She considered returning to a human village, but her very existence was tied to her coffin.

"That's when a man claiming to be Rostir's prime minister paid me a visit."

"?!"

"I could tell at first glance. He was a tremendously powerful demon."

Lithisia gripped her red shovel tightly, causing it to exude a blood-red aura. Alice cried out in fear.

"Your Royal Highness, you're scaring her. Please put away your shovel."

"I refuse, Catria. As a member of the royal family, it is my obligation to always keep my shovel on hand."

What an unnecessary obligation.

"Now, Alice. Continue. What did the prime minister shovel to you?"

"I'm pretty sure he didn't shovel anything," Catria interjected.

"If I corrupted the Blue Orb, he'd grant whatever wish I had," Alice somehow continued, on the verge of tears.

"Corrupted?"

"Deep in Veknar's knowledge is a type of magic known as an Ancient Curse. It requires the use of human sacrifices."

"Why would he want you to do that?"

"I know not. But as proof of our contract, he handed me this jewel," Alice explained as she pointed to the stone in her forehead.

The jewel in her head shone a creepy black.

"A diamond of the Dark World. Absolute proof of a contract with a higher demon." Alice sighed. "And so I faced you all in battle with the hopes of turning you into sacrifices, and ultimately lost. Nothing matters anymore... Wait, I take that back! No more shoveling, please!"

"...What do you mean, 'no more shoveling'?"

"Er, I mean shoveling is tremendous! All hail the shovel!"

"You finally get it?! Yay! All hail the shovel!"

"All hail the shovel!"

The two continued like this for a time.

"...So, Alice. Is that everything?"

"Yes. That's all there is to tell you."

"You left out the most important part."

Alan pointed his shovel at Alice's chest.

"What do *you* want?"

"Huh?"

The girl instantly stopped moving.

"You made a deal with the prime minister to get something, but you never told us what that something was."

"I-It has nothing to do with any of you."

"I'm asking because I want to know."

Alan was a miner. He lived to mine. The thought of letting a mystery remain forever buried went against his sense of self.

"Wh-who cares?! I don't have to tell you anything!"

Bling! Lithisia's red shovel shone.

"Please answer the question, Lady Alice."

"Ah! Aaaaaggggh! No, I refuse!" Despite being threatened by Lithisia's dreaded shovel, Alice shook her head from side to side.

"Shall we try a different, more intense kind of shoveling then?"

"AAAAAAAHHHHHH!!!"

Alice looked at Lithisia's shovel, then back at Alan. She lowered her head, and in a weak voice, said...

"...I wanted warmth."

Tears began to fall from her cheek and onto the ground.

"Warm food... Warm words... A warm bed..."

Alice continued.

"Not the cold chill of a dead body... I just wanted something warm."

She raised her face and reached her hand up toward the sun.

"Since the day I died 300 years ago..."

Despite being under the intense beams of the sun, Alice's body reflected none of its light. She was just as pale as she was deep within the castle.

"All I feel from the sun is a chill."

Catria and Alan were left without words as Alice finished telling her tale. Lithisia stared at the miner as though she'd come to a conclusion.

"Sir Miner... Is there any way you can bring Alice back to life with your powers?"

A few moments passed.

"I...can't."

Alan's words were laced with regret.

"A shovel can dig things up and bury them," he said as he pointed at the massive graveyard in front of them. "I may be able to bury the dead, but I can't bring them back to life."

"Is that...so..."

Lithisia's expression darkened, her voice growing quiet. Catria was in the same mental space. *You mean there's something this guy's shovel* can't *do?*

"I'm sorry. I'm not some god with power over death. My shovel has its limits..."

Alan gripped the shovel in his hand.

"At best, it can make someone with an astral body feel warmth, taste food, and move around freely without being tied to a coffin. And even that would only last for a hundred years."

Some time passed.

"I...see... Only 100 years...?"

"Yeah..."

Five seconds. 10 seconds. 20 seconds passed without anyone saying anything before Catria was forced to interject, as usual.

"Alan."

"What is it?"

"ISN'T THAT MORE THAN ENOUGH?!"

Why did Catria always have to play the straight man in these situations?

"W-w-w-wait just a second! Y-you can really do all of that?!" Alice had been sitting in silence the whole time, but could keep her mouth closed no longer.

"I mean, Lithisia did it earlier."

"Wha?"

"When she was tickling your feet with her shovel, did you not sweat profusely?"

"Oh my GOOOOOOOOD!!!"

Alan's shovel had the power to mine a person's senses from where they were buried deep within. For example, even if they weren't a physical being, it could still unearth the senses buried in their heart. Of course, Alice would have to subject herself to shovel tickling who knew how many times for this to work.

The whole coffin issue was much simpler. Alan could just walk around with it. The miner was especially good at carrying things.

"I see!"

Lithisia's eyes were shining.

"In other words, I just have to shovel Alice every day!"

"Wait, wait! Aren't we missing something important?!"

"Like what?"

"I-I mean, you guys have no obligation to save me."

"Actually, we do," responded Lithisia with a smile as radiant as the sun itself. "We're already shoveling buddies now!"

Alice's expression was one of both joy and fear. Nothing mattered anymore. Meanwhile, Catria simply watched the proceedings. She was a knight who knew how to read the room.

But then, Alice noticed something.

"My...hand..."

She had feeling in her hand for the first time in so many years. Even the tears falling from her eyes were warm.

"I..."

Immediately after.

OOOOOOOOOOOOOOOOOOOHHHHHHH-HHHHHHHHHHHH!

"...Ngh?! Alice, your forehead!"

The diamond from the Dark World. The jewel in her forehead that served as proof of her contract with a higher demon.

The black aura erupting from it was wrapping itself around Alice's body.

"I see... This is because I didn't hold up my end of the bargain..." Alice whispered as she ran her finger across the jewel.

"Alice! Your body!"

It was beginning to melt.

"Only death awaits those who do not hold up their end of the contract. It's only to be expected from a demon. But hey, I'm already dead, so all that's left is for me to disappear."

Despite the gravity of the situation, Alice seemed oddly at peace.

"No! This is too unfair! We were going to be shovel buddies!"

Even with things spiraling downward, the princess' mind was nonetheless filled with matters of shoveling.

"As if! Plus... I'm okay now," Alice said with a smile. It was the gentlest smile of the day.

She once again reached up for the sun, then looked at Lithisia.

"I'm finally warm."

Just as Lithisia broke down into tears...

"DIG!"

Alan leapt into action.

His shovel smashed into the black diamond in Alice's forehead with incomprehensible speed. An aura of blue energy surrounded the tool, and like a talented jeweler removing a precious rock from a ring, Alan plucked out the diamond.

Thunk.

The black diamond rolled along the ground. The dark aura surrounding it was still attempting to make its way toward Alice, so Alan smashed it with his shovel once more, burying it deep underground. Just like with the Dark Beasts, he had buried the diamond some 10,000 meters beneath the surface and sealed it away.

This Shovel Seal was unbreakable even by the emperor of hell itself. A higher demon's curse would stand no chance.

"?!"

"Didn't I tell you?"

Alice looked up at Alan, the man bathed in the light of the sun. He shone more brightly than the sun itself.

"My shovel digs, and it buries."

Alice couldn't look away from Alan. All she could do was continue to stare at the hero who had saved her from the depths of despair.

As promised, the party made a trip back to the elf castle to tell Fio all about what had transpired. She could barely hold back her own tears.

"Amazing... I'm just so overcome by all this weirdness."

"Hrm. What part of the story was weird?"

"All of it, duh!" Catria interjected, still internally asking herself what a shovel was. "...By the way, where's the princess?"

"She's shoveling Alice."

"Ah, got it." The knight had given up trying to intercede.

"Stop it! You're not supposed to dig anything up from there!"

"That's not true. There's no spot on a girl that shouldn't be shoveled."

Catria could hear the young girl's screams, but chose to pretend she couldn't. The princess finally had a friend to shovel with, and Catria wanted nothing to do with it. Instead, she turned back to the miner to discuss continuing their journey.

"Alan, our next destination is the desert." According to Lithisia, the Red Orb was buried within a pyramid in the desert.

"The desert, eh? Perfect." Alan grinned. Catria could already picture his next words.

"It's shoveling time."

The Rubbing of Alice

THAT NIGHT, Alan thought back on his earlier conversation with Fio. He'd asked if she wanted to tag along with them on their quest, and Fio had given it serious thought before deciding to stay behind and work on reviving the Elf Woods. Her new goal in life was to restore the once-thriving forest to what it used to be.

"I'm going to do my best and see this through to the end. So, um… Uncle Alan, I'll be waiting for you here."

Fio had squirmed a bit before looking up at Alan, wearing the expression of someone who had something to say, but couldn't quite find the words.

"I understand. I plan on swinging by every once in a while and help out."

"Th-thank you so much!" Fio said with a big smile, bowing her head up and down.

"That being said, all I can really do is physical labor."

"Aaaaah! Physical labor?!"

Fio's face suddenly turned bright red. She looked down at the floor and began to squirm, rubbing her voluptuous thighs together.

"O-okay... I'm looking forward to, um, experiencing your physical labor," she said with a smile.

Why was she blushing? Alan thought to himself, but could arrive at no answer. He was as dense as they came.

Then came a knock. Someone was at his door. Alan opened it to find Alice, still not wearing a stitch of clothing.

"G-good evening..." she said.

A chill immediately ran down the miner's spine. Déjà vu. Did Lithisia put her up to this? "Are you here to shovel?"

"What?! Y-you're going to shovel me, too?!"

"No! As long as you don't want me to, I won't." Alan had never been more glad to be wrong.

"O-oh, thank goodness..." Alice fell to her knees, relieved. "Please, listen. I tried to sleep in a warm bed for the first time in forever."

"Mm. You deserve it."

"But then Lithisia came crashing into the room with shovel in hand, smiling and saying 'Shovely, shovely!' ... Please, I beg of you. Let me hide in here!"

The undead queen was on her hands and knees, pleading to Alan, and there was no way he'd refuse. Especially given how she was trembling in fear.

"Sure," he said. "I don't mind."

"Thank you! Thank you so much! I'm saved!"

Alice looked even happier than she did when she felt the warmth of the sun on her skin the other day.

"But are you sure you wanna stick with me? What about Catria?"

"She's a servant to the princess, is she not? Plus, when I'm near her, my body gets all hot... It's scary."

"Ah, that must be the power of her Holy Knight Shovel." Alan had poured Divine Shovel Power into Catria's shovel. Unbeknownst to Catria, like the safety first helmet, it would gradually empower its wielder with Divine Shovel Power over time. An undead creature like Alice would certainly find her unsettling.

Alan decided to let Alice use the bed, setting up camp on the floor himself. The carpeting in the elf castle was nice and warm thanks to the heating system, which utilized magma from hell.

"Er..."

"Is something wrong?"

"N-no, I, well, erm... Never mind. It's nothing. I guess."

Alice was clearly lying. Alan felt her glancing at him time and time again. In fact, upon closer inspection, she was lying dramatically close to one edge of the bed.

In other words...

"You want me to sleep next to you, eh?"

"?!"

She was very easy to read.

"I-I-I'm the queen of the undead! As if I would ever crave the warmth of another!"

"It's fine, let's just sleep."

"Aaaaah! But Catria said you were super d-dense!"

It made perfect sense that a young girl who had spent hundreds of years yearning for warmth would desire a replacement for her parents. Alan scooped Alice up in his arms and got in bed. Once in bed, he slowly patted her head. Alice grimaced.

"I'm... I'm not a child... Ah..."

But her tone betrayed her true feelings.

"Just be quiet and enjoy this. As far as I'm concerned, you're still a child."

"I may look like one, but I've been alive for at least 333 years. I am Veknar's successor and queen of the undead."

"Well I'm 1,011 years old, so."

"What kind of absurd joke is that...?"

"It's true."

He continued to rub her head.

"If there's anything you want me to do, just let me know."

"Er, no, I... I most definitely don't want you to hold me."

"Gotcha."

Alan brought his hand down to her astral body's stomach. It was warm. In an attempt to transmit some of his warmth into Alice, he gently caressed her skin.

"Gyaaah! You-you perv! This is against the law!"

"Weren't you just saying you were 333 years old?"

Despite her words, Alice showed no signs of resisting his touch. With every brush of his hand against her skin, her cheeks grew slightly more pink. She was probably extra sensitive thanks to Lithisia's shoveling. Her toes were shaking, too. She must've been enjoying this quite a bit.

When she finally spoke, her voice sounded strangely relieved.

"What am I going to do now...?"

"Just do whatever you want. You're free."

"Kind of an irresponsible thing to say, considering you did this to me."

"Sorry, but I can't tell other people how to live out their lives."

Alan was just a miner. His only desire was to unearth buried things up, and that desire dictated everything he did. How could someone like that tell another person how to live their life? All he could really do was help them walk their path.

"You're the one who has to decide what's next, Alice."

"...I know." She nodded her head and then started to laugh. "I guess even you can act like a normal human sometimes."

"Hrm? What's that supposed to mean? I'm perfectly normal all the time."

"Yeah, right." Alice's eyes were slowly sliding shut. "My goal..."

"Didn't you say you wanted warmth?"

"I think I'm...okay now..." She gripped Alan back, tightly. "I can't think of anything else..."

That was to be expected. She'd been granted a brand-new lease on life when she least expected it. "And that's fine. You have plenty of time to think it over. Heck, I've been thinking about it for 1,000 years."

"...Okay."

It wasn't long before Alan could hear Alice's quiet breathing even out.

"Mm... Father...." she murmured in her sleep. Finally, she looked her age.

Could Alan really be the father figure that this girl so desired? Would that make Lithisia her mother? That'd spell bad news for her upbringing. Either way, he saved this girl's life, and he would now do everything in his power to help her live it.

"Mm?! Aaaah, no! Noooo!" Alice's expression began to twist and contort as she shook her head wildly.

Was she having a nightmare?

"No! No more shovels! It doesn't feel good when you rub my ears like...that..."

It was in fact a nightmare.

A true nightmare (important enough to say twice).

▷━━━━▶

"And so that's what went down last night." On the road to the desert nation the next day, Alan spilled the beans about the previous night's events.

"Why are you telling them?!"

"I see! So you got shoveled by Sir Miner, too!" Lithisia was happy that another girl had joined her, uh, sisterhood.

"You've got it all wrong! We just slept together! There was no shoveling involved!"

"I call that the Sleepy Shovel! We should try it, too!"

"Alan! Alan! I beg of you, do something about this crazy shovel lady!"

"Sorry, no can do."

There were things a shovel could and couldn't do. Fixing Lithisia was first in the latter category.

"Alan, we'll be hitting the border of Desertopia momentarily," Catria interjected, ignoring Alice's plight. Like the miner, she had also given up all hope of fixing the princess.

"Their borders are guarded, right?"

"Correct. They have a poor relationship with our nation."

"Don't abandon me! Pleaaaaase!"

Still ignoring Alice's cries for help, Catria went on to explain that Desertopia was a military nation located to the northwest of Rostir. Most of its land was composed of desert, but the areas around its multiple oases were used as farmland. Its formidable military made it an apex predator, and it expanded its territory through waging war. Its relationship with Rostir, as a result, was incredibly rocky.

"Hrm, I can think of three ways in," Alan said with confidence.

"I'd rather not hear you out, but go ahead."

"The first way is to shovel up all the sand in the desert. The second is to fly through the air using my shovel. The third is to build a shovel battleship on the surface and blow up the checkpoint."

Sizzle. That was the sound of Catria's brain overheating, and it wasn't the sun's fault. It was working at maximum capacity to try and understand Alan's words.

"...Alan, no more jokes. This is a serious problem."

"I'm not joking."

Catria sighed. He wasn't joking. What the heck was a shovel battleship?!

"And wait, you can fly?"

"Of course I can."

"'Of course', he says..."

"I basically straddle my shovel and fire out Shovel Power to propel myself through the air."

"Don't you 'basically' me! None of that makes sense."

"But we do have a problem with these three options."

"A problem? I'd say we have more than that."

"They're all attention-getting. We'd be stoking direct conflict with all of Desertopia."

"Hrm, so even the great Alan is scared of Desertopia's military might, eh?" Catria seemed almost pleased by the prospect, but the miner shook his head from side to side.

"I'm fully confident that I could wipe out their entire military on my own..."

"Oh."

"You're shovely amazing, Sir Miner!"

"This is the man who annihilated my undead army in five seconds..."

"...but if I did that, I wouldn't be able to do business with them going forward," Alan finished. He was a jewel miner, which meant he needed people to sell his jewels to. "Let's do this stealthily. Time to change our looks."

"Excellent! A sensible plan for once!" Catria exclaimed, then trailed off as Alan lifted his shovel and pointed it at himself. "Er, what are you doing?"

"I'm going to disguise myself using my shovel."

"Excuse me?"

Alan covered his face with the metal portion of the shovel. When he pulled it away, he had become Fio. His entire body, hair, face, and gender now perfectly mirrored the elf girl, down to the most minute detail.

"GHAAAAAARGGHHHHLEEEE?!" Catria screamed like a banshee.

"Shoveling shoveltastic!" Translation: Sir Miner is the bestest!

"No, no, no, no! C'mon! This isn't even a disguise

anymore!" Alan had *become* a beautiful elf girl. Why didn't anyone else find this extremely bizarre?!

"There's nothing strange about this. A shovel can dig things up, and it can bury them."

"Your point?!"

"I 'buried' my face and transformed," Alan stated with confidence.

Sizzle, sizzle. Catria's brain was being deep fried in a vat of oil.

"Now come, Catria. I'm going to transform you."

"Wow! I bet all kinds of hot shovel experiences await us inside!"

Ah, Catria thought to herself, *Desertopia is doomed.*

Wave Motion Shovel Blast

Special Move

EXPLANATION

Alan's special attack, which utilizes the repeated actions of digging and burying to produce wave energy that he can use to fire a beam. Has the power to destroy planets.

MAXIMUM TARGETS

All of humanity (approximately 7 billion people).

DAMAGE

Base: 100d100 (Expected number: 5050)
Depending on the level and Shovel Power, the number of die changes.

ATTRIBUTES

Wave Motion + Earth + Chaos + Pure Magical Energy + Shovel.
If the target is vulnerable to one or more of these attributes, it will take full damage.

SPECIAL EFFECTS

When a direct hit is landed on an enemy, they will be afflicted with one of the following status effects: Inhume, Excavation, Love, Insta-Death, or Causal Confusion. These status effects do not heal over time. Which of these status effects the target is inflicted with is determined by the game master or the person who fired the Wave Motion Shovel Blast in the first place.

HOLY SHOVEL EMPIRE, OFFICIAL DICTIONARY
(AUTHOR: LITHISIA), 7TH VERSION.

CHAPTER 3

The Desert
Nation's Shovel
(JULIA'S INTRODUCTION)

PART 12
The Miner Saves Julia, the Water Priestess

AND SO, Alan's party infiltrated Desertopia.
But not without incident.

The group had disguised themselves as traveling shovelists (excuse me?) in order to pass through the checkpoint. But Lithisia went berserk after one of the guards made fun of shovels, and Alan was forced to use his Wave Motion Shovel Blast to annihilate said checkpoint. Since the military immediately mobilized in response, the miner created a path through the desert for them to escape. A path leading directly from the border to the capital city.

It only took Alan five seconds to create this twenty-kilometer path.

"I know I destroyed the checkpoint and all, but since I made a path to the capital, I'd say we're about even."

"Your sense of balance is wonderful, just like a square shovel!"

"About even?! Are you kidding me?!" Catria looked at the massive stone path stretching out to the end of the desert and sighed.

Who the heck is this guy?!

This was already the eighth time she'd asked that question today.

"Hrm, so this is the modern capital city, eh? Impressive," whispered Alice, a childlike smile on her face.

"It's been three hundred years since I last saw the world... I wonder how it's changed."

Lithisia shuffled close to Alan. "Sir Miner, Alice looks really happy."

Indeed. Despite what happened yesterday with Lithisia and her shovel, the girl seemed full of life. Her conversation with Alan must have given her a lot to think about.

"Hee hee, if she's this lively now, we can shovel until the cows come home!"

"Eek!"

"Stop playing around. We're about to enter the capital."

Needless to say, the security in the capital was much tighter than at the checkpoint, but Alan managed to circumvent all of that by digging a tunnel under the castle walls in point two seconds. This was clearly something no human should've been capable of, but the party had long since grown used to his absurdity.

Just beyond the tunnel was a bustling marketplace. A myriad of merchants, all wearing turbans, loudly advertised their wares.

"Amazing! I'd heard that the markets in Desertopia were something else." Lithisia's eyes were drawn every which way. "Sir Miner, Sir Miner! They're selling lots of children's clothes over there!"

"...Do you want some?"

"Yeah! I wanna dress Alice up in all sorts of outfits and shovel her up."

Alice (usually invisible to the eyes of others) let out an exasperated sigh. "Because I have an astral body, anything I wear becomes see-through."

"Hee hee, is that so...? All the better to shovel with... Shrool..."

That was her way of combining "shovel" with "drool." The princess was getting creative.

"Let us make some purchases! Come now, Alice."

"Gah! Don't touch me! I'll go with you, just don't touch me with that shovel of yours!"

"I'll accompany to guard the princess."

"There's no need for that. Alice is 300 times stronger than you are."

"Urgh..."

Alan wasn't being cruel, he was merely speaking the truth. 300 Catria stood no chance against the undead queen. While she looked like a young girl, she had inherited a tremendous amount of power from Veknar, the strongest of the liches.

"Plus, I lack common sense. I need someone like you around to help me."

"So you admit to it?!"

"I'm a miner, after all."

"You ought to apologize to all the miners out there."

And so, Lithisia and Alice went one way, while Catria and Alan went in search of information about the orb. It was then that Alan's eyes landed upon something. Someone, in fact.

A slave.

Standing on a wooden platform were women and children in tattered clothes.

"The slave trade. Apparently, it's totally legal in Desertopia," Catria explained.

"What's the point in owning a slave?"

"They can carry things, clean, do heavy lifting... All kinds of simple work."

"Why not just simply use a shovel?"

"Do you even hear yourself?"

Alan looked at the slaves lined up on the platform. One in particular caught his eye. "Even that girl is a slave?"

Unlike the other slaves, the girl in question was wearing clothes made of thin, white fabric, and had blue hair so beautiful that it rivaled even Lithisia's. She had a slender nose, and her skin was blindingly white. Hanging from her neck was a sign with a price tag.

And then there were her breasts, which were massive. There was even some underboob action going on, due to her current attire.

"Come one, come all! We've uncovered the biggest treasure of the year! Julia the dancer!" When the merchant clapped his hands together, all eyes focused on the girl. Immediately noticing the lewd eyes honing in on her chest, the girl tried to cover it from view. Despite being in handcuffs, she moved with grace and elegance.

"Hey, stop covering up! You got great tits, so show 'em off to the audience!"

"Ah... Okay... I'm so sorry..." Julia followed the slave merchant's orders and brought her arms down. "My apologies..."

Each time she apologized, she gripped something tightly. It was some kind of glass bottle filled with water.

"Alan, what are you looking at?" Catria asked. She looked annoyed. "What, you want a slave or something? She your type?"

"No, I don't want a slave. My Shovel Senses are reacting to that girl."

"Speak human, please."

"She has the aura of someone with 'something' buried deep within her."

"You mean she's got some sort of incredible talent or something? I suppose she does have that sort of aura." Even ignoring her obvious beauty, the way she moved was hypnotizing.

"Thank you for your patronage!" The slave merchant clapped his hands together, and a broadly built, middle-aged man walked on stage. He had apparently bought Julia.

"Huh... Ah..." Scared but powerless to resist, Julia simply cried out in fear.

"Oh ho ho... Hrm? What's this glass bottle?" The man grabbed it from Julia's hand.

"That's... No!!!"

"What's yours is mine, slave. Hah. I'll be taking this."

"N-no, please..."

Julia stretched her arm out. Whatever the bottle was, it was clearly important to her.

"It's just water? Whatever. I'll use the bottle for my own drinks." The large man immediately emptied the water out onto the ground in front of the girl.

"Ah... The Water of Rahal..."

Tears began to take shape in Julia's eyes as she collapsed to her knees.

"I'm so sorry... I'm so sorry, everyone..."

Her new owner violently grabbed her by the neck and drew her close, bringing his hand near her ample breasts. He was clearly thinking something terrible.

"Human trash." Catria was already reaching for the sword on her back. Julia may have been a slave, but Catria would be a failure of a knight if she didn't stand up for a young girl being shamed in front of a large crowd like this. "Aren't you going to do something, Alan?"

Despite the whole shovel thing, she'd thought he had a real sense of justice. Just as she was beginning to feel disappointed, Alan answered.

"I already have."

A moment later—

KA-CHOOOOOOOOM!

A massive hole opened up in the platform.

"GYAAAAAAAHH!"

The middle-aged man screamed in terror as he plummeted from view. For tens of seconds, there was no confirmation of him reaching the bottom of the hole, but finally, everyone present heard the distant splash of water. Alan tapped the hole on the wooden platform with his shovel, and it shone brightly before closing up.

"Wha? B-but, what about the hole…?"

"Fear not. I just dug one up with my shovel."

"Excuse me?"

"I didn't take his life. I dropped him into an underground water vein."

"Excuse me?!"

"Did you really think that explanation would float with a normal person?!" Despite her words, Catria wore a smile on her face.

What was I thinking? This is who he is. I know he can be a pain in the butt at times, but this shoveling jerk has a real sense of justice.

"Wh-what just happened!? What in blazes did you do?! Guards!"

The slave merchant rang a bell and the customers immediately dispersed, allowing capable-looking warriors wielding falchions to flood in. There were about 50 in total, and most already had bows and arrows trained on Alan.

"Ah… Ah…" Julia instinctively approached Alan. She was clearly panicked. "P-please run… You don't stand a chance against them."

Alan was moved. Despite being in mortal danger, this girl was concerned for his life.

"Don't worry, I plan on running. But you're coming with me. I'm sending you home."

Julia quietly shook her head from side to side.

"No." Her intent was clear. "I'm going to stay here. I can act as a distraction."

"You'll die."

"Maybe... But I don't have a home to go back to anymore..." Julia explained weakly, her decision seemingly final.

"I don't know what your deal is, but I'm guessing I won't be convincing you one way or the other."

"I'm sorry... Please take care, kind sir."

"Which means I gotta do this my way."

KA-CHOOMDOOGLESHAAAAAM!!!

A flash of light erupted from Alan's shovel. Just like that, Julia's handcuffs and legcuffs were destroyed.

"Huh?! Wh-what did you just... Aaah!"

Alan silently lifted Julia up into his arms. He wasn't taking no for an answer. Elsewhere, Catria quietly chuckled.

"You can't! Put me down! I'm a sinner! I'm not worth saving!"

"A sinner?"

"I... I betrayed everyone and fled from my village..." Tears ran down her cheeks. "I was scared of being the Water Priestess, so I ran... I just ran..."

"Don't worry. I may not know the details of what happened, but I'll go with you and apologize, too."

"You can't... I've done something I can't undo..." Julia looked down at the ground. "And... And I've lost the proof that I'm the Water Priestess..."

The proof she spoke of was the Water of Rahal, which her owner poured out onto the ground only moments ago. The liquid had already been absorbed into the sand. There would be no reclaiming it.

"I can't ever get that water back..."

Julia continued to weep.

"Hrm." Alan had a solid grasp of the situation now, and he knew that Julia believed she'd never be forgiven for her sins. Which meant that the first thing he had to do was clear up one of her misconceptions.

"Julia, right? Let me correct you."

"Huh...?"

"You're right. *You* can't ever get that water back. However."

Alan gripped his shovel with one hand.

"DIG!"

The ground split into two, and from the crack emerged a lump of earth about the size of a house. It was the same ground that had absorbed the Water of Rahal only moments ago.

Alan focused his energy into his shovel. He was going to activate Time Shovel. This technique allowed him to reverse the flow of time in an object to a certain point. As time began to march back, so too did the flow of the Water of Rahal.

And just like that, Julia's bottle was full again.

"Wh-what...?"

She stared in shock at the glass bottle, clueless as to what had just transpired.

"With a shovel, *I* can absolutely get that water back."

"Huh?"

The slave girl was still unclear about pretty much everything.

"Alan! The guards are coming!" shouted Catria. Alan nodded.

ROOOOOAAAAAR!

Responding to Alan's Shovel Power, the air in the desert roared as the wind whipped up into a fury. The aura surrounding his shovel grew bigger and bigger until it surpassed the size of a human, eventually reaching for the heavens.

"DIG!"

KAA-ZOOOOOOOOSH!"

Fifty different beams of light exploded from the shovel, firing in all directions. This was Alan's Shotgun Wave Motion Shovel Blast. Instead of firing a single beam in one direction, it fired multiple homing beams. The beams sank into the ground under the guards' feet, immediately creating holes that they then fell into.

"?!"

Julia was more confused than she had been in her entire life, but that was only to be expected. There wasn't a single human on the planet who wouldn't be confused by the Shotgun Wave Motion Shovel Blast.

"See, Julia? With my shovel..." Alan paused. "I can save your spilled water. The Water of Rahal? No sweat. Your village? No problem? You? Absolutely."

Julia stared at Alan in dumbfounded silence. Everything she knew about the world had been turned upside down in the span of minutes. *Who... Who is this man?! What is he?!*

Watching from a distance, Catria sighed. *Looks like today's sacrifice is this Water Priestess.*

PART 13

The Miner Drinks the Water Priestess's Shovel Water

THE CARRIAGE, which was large enough to hold about 10 people, rocked to and fro in the desert. After kicking the ever-loving stuffing out of the slave merchant, Lithisia had gone ahead and swiped his horse and carriage as things started to get messy. The plan was to head back to Julia's hometown, and Alice and Catria were handling the actual driving while Alan and Lithisia stayed with Julia in the back.

"So now we're carriage thieves, eh? I know we had no choice and all, but..."

"Incorrect, Sir Miner. We aren't thieves. I made sure to leave behind a shovel."

"...Like a calling card?"

"No, as payment of course!"

There was nothing "of course" about her statement, but Lithisia seemed wholly satisfied.

"So, Julia. I think it's about time you explain to us what's going on."

"I'm a part of the Rahal Tribe... I was going to undergo the Ritual of Water Summoning."

According to Julia, the Ritual of Water Summoning wasn't just ceremonial, but a kind of magic in and of itself. The reason Desertopia had become such a massive nation was because of its oases. In order to make sure they didn't dry up, generations of Water Priestesses would undergo the Ritual of Water Summoning. Said Water Priestesses were worshipped as deity-like beings.

"And you're one of them, Lady Julia?"

"Yes... Or at least, I was..."

Lithisia nodded her head, clearly fascinated by the girl's tale. "A ritual, huh? We could use one of those... Just think. A Ritual of Shovel Summoning? A Shovtual?"

Her thought process was heading in an unfortunate direction.

"Er, um, what are you talking about?"

"Shovel teachings, of course."

Julia's expression went blank. "Um, Sir Alan? Who exactly is this young lady?"

"Oh, right. I forgot to introduce you. Lithisia."

"Of course!" The princess curtsied formally. "I'm the High Priestess of the Holy Shovel Faith, Lithisia."

"Are you kidding me?"

Alan wasn't sure where to start.

"I'm also the first princess of Rostir!"

"Take this seriously, please."

"I'm shoveled to make your acquaintance!"

A new greeting? "Just shut up, please."

"Um, er... A High Priestess and a princess? Um, um, um..." Julia's voice was filled with confusion. Of course it was. Even Alan was confused.

"Julia, just ignore everything she said."

"B-but...."

"As Sir Miner has said, all is shovely!"

Julia tilted her head, still very much puzzled. As expected from one called the Water Priestess, she had a heart as pure as water itself. Alan would have to take great care to make sure that she wasn't corrupted.

"So the head of the Rahal Tribe knows a lot about legends, yeah?"

"Correct. The pyramid was initially a legend passed down within the Rahal Tribe."

They weren't just accompanying Julia back to her village as an act of kindness. This was a chance to obtain information on their next objective, the Red Orb.

"By the way, Lady Julia. Is the Ritual of Water Summoning a kind of dance?"

"It is. It's a dance passed down within the tribe."

"Do you think you could show me? I'd love to see it!"

Julia shook her head sadly. "I'm...no longer a priestess, so..."

"You said you ran off. What happened?"

Julia swallowed loudly and nodded her head.

Several years ago, at the end of a series of arduous trials, Julia had inherited the title of Water Priestess. Yet, when she first performed the Ritual of Water Summoning, the water levels actually dropped. The head of the tribe and the rest of the village believed that the priestess' dance had angered the dragon.

"Angered the dragon?"

"The 'Despair Devouring Dragon' that turned this land into a desert long ago."

According to the legend, the dragon burned away all of modern civilization in a single night, feeding on humanity's despair. The very first Water Priestess calmed the angry beast, and it sank into a deep sleep. The pyramid was its resting place, and the Rahal Tribe the ancestors of the original priestess.

Julia had failed to execute the ritual properly, which was why she was originally headed for the pyramid to begin with—to atone for her sins. As recorded in the legends, she would need to sacrifice herself to the dragon in order to calm its anger.

"!!!"

Julia began to tremble a little.

She was supposed to become a sacrifice, and yet here she was with Alan and the others. That in and of itself was a sin, and the very reason she no longer had the right to call herself the Water Priestess.

"You ran from the dragon."

"I..."

The trembling grew more intense.

"I heard it... I heard the dragon's voice... It said, 'I shall devour you.'"

Julia continued with her confession.

"I thought I was ready. I thought I was prepared to surrender my life, but when I heard its voice, all of that conviction vanished into thin air. All I could do was run as fast as I could, crying. I just kept running and running across the desert...!"

She could never return to her village again. Not only had she failed to summon water, she'd run from her responsibility. She was worthless.

I should die, she thought to herself.

"And then you were caught by a slave merchant?"

Lithisia was holding back her own tears. "This must've been so hard for you... It's such a shovelingly sad story..."

"You and your shovel need to keep quiet. But hrm, a dragon, eh?"

Alan thought to himself. Julia didn't run away from being a sacrifice because she feared death. Dragon speech had magical properties that allowed them to control the hearts of others. It was likely that Julia had encountered the dragon, fallen under the beast's control, and instinctively escaped.

"I get it now. But..."

There was still one unclear portion of this little tale.

"Did you really fail?"

"...Huh?"

"Did your ritual really fail? It went fine during practice, did it not?" Alan hadn't yet seen her dance in person, but he could tell based on the way she handled herself that she was a very skilled dancer. "Is it possible that somebody interfered with the ritual?"

"Huh? Um, no... The village elder made sure everything went as planned."

"The village elder, eh?"

Julia nodded again. "Surely, I must have made a mistake..."

"We might be able to find out why that happened."

"Wha?! Really?! But how??"

"When it comes to water, I know my stuff."

Digging tunnels to manipulate the flow of water was an important aspect of Alan's job. In that sense, he and Julia had similar skills.

"The reason the water level dropped..."

"Could you dance the Ritual of Water Summoning for me?"

Julia's eyes were clearly sparkling, and that made Alan as happy as could be. She hadn't lost her passion. Not yet. She was filled with the drive to mine for water, the jewel of the desert. She was very much like Alan, in that way.

"B-but, I... I... Haaah." Julia's hands were shaking. She was so aware of her own sins that she couldn't bring herself to take that all-important step forward.

"Lady Julia, I know a great spell to calm your nerves!"

"You do?"

Lithisia began to gently whisper in Julia's ear. The Water Priestess closed her eyes and began to whisper something herself.

"A-a-all hail Alan... All hail S-Sir Alan... All hail the mighty shovel..."

Or something to that effect.

"Lithisia. What exactly are you making her do?"

"A prayer to help her get back on her feet."

"You're just having her say my name. You really think that's going to work?"

"Of course it will. What do you think, Lady Julia?" Lithisia asked with confidence.

Julia took a deep breath and opened her eyes.

"Um, I feel a little better... I think."

"Seriously?!"

Julia actually did look like she'd calmed down a bit.

"H-how mysterious..."

"Um, I... I don't have any faith in myself, but..." The young girl gripped her bottle. "Sir Alan, you made a miracle happen. You saved the water that I had lost. I feel like I can have faith in your mighty words..."

"How shovely wonderful! Lady Julia, you have exactly what it takes to become a Shovel Priestess!"

There was nothing left for Alan to say.

"So, um, I think I can dance now..." Julia said cheerfully. "E-excuse me..."

Julia slowly rose to her feet and began to dance. She looked almost weightless. Her breasts bounced up and down as her slim figure smoothly transitioned between movements. She looked up toward the heavens, then lowered her face, praying for water like a priestess should.

Eventually, Alan even smelled water.

"That's all."

Clap, clap, clap, clap. Clank, clank, clank, clank. Lithisia applauded with all of her might. The clanking noise came from the shovel hitting the floor. "Amazing! Positively amazing! That was a true shovel dance!"

Lithisia's words were as indecipherable as ever, but she was right in that Julia's work was truly that of a professional. The dancer had put everything she had into her performance, and even Alan could see that. Heck, there was proof.

"Looks like it wasn't your fault the ritual failed."

"Huh?!"

"Look at this."

Alan raised his shovel. Sitting atop its head was a pool of water. It had appeared during Julia's dance.

"You summoned this water."

"I did?!"

"Sir Miner, what kind of shovel science is this?"

"I made some adjustments so that the water summoning Shovel Power from within Julia would manifest and gather atop the shovel. If she was able to summon this much water in such a short period of time, I can't imagine her dance being the problem. Plus..."

Alan dipped his finger into the water and licked it. The flavor was delightfully sweet and addictive. It was water that made one think of Julia's sweetness and purity.

"It tastes fantastic. Julia executed the ritual perfectly."

"I see... So this is Lady Julia's shovel juice, then?"

"E-excuse me?!"

Julia held herself, clearly embarrassed by Lithisia's phrasing. Oblivious to this, Lithisia dipped her finger into the water and took a taste as well. "Lady Julia's water really is delicious! Aaah..."

"U-um, please don't react so intensely..." The Water Priestess' cheeks had turned pink as she squirmed about. She was happy, but embarrassed. Embarrassed beyond belief.

"Your water really is a treat," Alan said. Julia had lost faith in herself, which meant he needed to take this chance to boost her confidence as much as possible.

"Aaaah..." For the first time in her life, Julia felt a certain strange emotion. They were only drinking her water, so why? Why was this so embarrassing?

Alan drank the last of the water she had summoned. "Mm, delicious. This is proof that you're a real deal Water Priestess."

"I shovely feel the same way."

Julia panted heavily. "Nngh..."

As Alan joyfully swallowed the last bit of water, her expression changed. She was genuinely proud of herself.

"Let's have everyone in your tribe try some of this."

After a pause, Julia nodded her head as tears of joy streamed down her face. "Thank you... Thank you so much..."

"Sir Alan, isn't it about time you find out where the village... Whoa! What the hell?!"

Catria reentered the carriage, doing a double take at the sight that met her eyes. Alan and Lithisia were smiling broadly, a soaked shovel in the former's hands, and Julia was panting heavily while crying and offering words of gratitude.

"What the hell is going on in here?!"

"Oh, we just had some of Lady Julia's shovel juice that she summoned with her shovel dance."

"They...drank me dry," Julia said, her cheeks bright red.

Catria took a moment to think before sighing deeply.

Everything about this is strange, but I suppose that's nothing new. Whatever.

PART 14

The Princess Acquires 58 New Shovel Believers

THE RAHAL TRIBE'S VILLAGE was small, and located in the center of the desert. The villagers themselves were mostly garbed in what seemed to be rags, but that wasn't the first thing that Alan noticed. No, it was their eyes. They looked dead.

"This is awful."

They looked even worse for wear than Julia did when she was a slave. The villagers were crouched on the ground, staring into the distance. They showed no signs of either moving or wanting to move.

"This whole oasis drying up thing... Is the problem really that pressing?"

"Water... Water is our life force," Julia struggled to answer. "This is my fault..."

Alan plopped his hand on her head. "Don't worry. I'm going to figure out why the ritual failed."

Julia looked up at Alan with pleading eyes.

"Oh, right. Julia, you should learn how to dig up water with a shovel."

"Huh? But I'm a priestess. I don't need a shovel."

"Priestesses and shovels. Prieshovel. See? They go together perfectly."

What is wrong with you? Catria thought to herself. That said, she didn't try to intervene. It was pointless.

After thinking for a minute, Julia nodded. She wasn't sure she followed what Alan was saying, but she decided to believe in him nonetheless. "All right... Sir Alan, please teach me how to dig."

"Mm. Then let's start by looking for a water source."

Alan tapped the ground with his shovel and pressed it into the dirt. By focusing his energies into the shovel like this, it would resonate with the water hidden beneath the surface, allowing him to locate any water sources within 50 kilometers.

When he explained this to Julia, she simply shook her head from side to side.

"I'm sorry, um... I have no clue what you just did..."

Catria felt exactly the same. This miner constantly ignored the rules of nature.

"No worries. You have the right qualities for this, Julia. You'll be able to learn how to do this in no time at all. I know this for a fact. After all, you made that sweet and delicious Julia Water."

The girl's cheeks went red again. As embarrassing as it was to have a type of water with her name, it also made her happy.

But then...

"Hrm... There's no water nearby?" Alan could hardly believe it. It was as if some great heat had steamed away all the oases in the area. Someone was responsible for this.

He felt the presence of something dark.

"Julia! You've returned!" A surprised voice echoed throughout the village. When the party turned around, they beheld an older man with feather ornaments in his hair and a stern expression on his face. This was the village elder.

"Village Elder, I..."

"No excuses. You traitorous priestess! Have you no shame showing your face here?"

"..." Julia trembled, on the verge of tears.

"Lady Julia! The shovel! Remember the way of the shovel!"

Lithisia's bizarre words of encouragement caused Julia to stop in her tracks.

"Ah, oh mighty shovel... Sir Alan, please grant me courage! Alaaan!" Somehow, this little prayer helped Julia muster her courage once again. "Please l-listen to... what I have to s-say, Village Elder."

"Excuse me?"

Julia clasped her hands tightly before her as she desperately pleaded with the man. "I was able to summon water e-earlier. So I... I think there's another reason why the oasis dried up..."

"Hrmph, nonsense. Nothing but excuses!"

"Village Elder, um, I—"

"You brought disaster upon our village. This time, you will be sacrificed as planned. Come."

Julia's expression darkened with despair and great sadness. When trust was broken, it couldn't be recovered. Just like spilled water.

"This is ridiculous!" Catria raised her voice. "Alan, don't you think this is awful?"

"Of course I do."

"Then..."

"Yeah, I know."

Alan held his shovel up.

There was a single flash of light—

And the village elder's head went flying. There was no blood. Instead, the elder's head flew through the air, feathers and all. It eventually smashed into one of the nearby tents and rolled to the ground.

All that remained was his body and those who had gathered nearby.

"…"

Julia was completely frozen, as were the rest of the villagers. It took five seconds before Catria could react.

"You bastard, what have you dooooooone?!" she shouted. *His head went flying! The elder's head went flying! You completely ignored the rules of engagement!*

"All I did was take his head off with my shovel."

"Exactly! You're not supposed to do that to people!" *Yes, that was awesome! Sure! But now you're an actual murderer!*

"That's where you're wrong. I'm no murderer."

"Are you out of your mind?!"

"Catria, aren't people supposed to bleed after getting beheaded?"

He was right.

The man's head had been taken clear off, but there was no blood to be seen. Catria had initially assumed that this was due to the sharpness of the shovel, but that was just because she, too, had had her brain corrupted by Alan and his shovel madness. Now that she thought about it, it was clearly very strange.

By the time Catria realized this, the elder's body began to emit a hissing sound, like it was filled with boiling water.

"Cursed human, how did you know?" A sinister voice filled the air, emanating from no identifiable source.

"My shovel power."

"Bwahahaha! Humans say the most foolish things."

"I'm not joking."

When Alan went searching for water veins earlier, he had sensed a dark presence and identified it as belonging to a powerful demon. From there, it had been easy to figure out what was going on. The elder was actually a Doppelganger, a demon capable of transforming itself to mimic the physical appearance of its targets.

"I have two questions. Where's the real elder? And what's your objective?"

"Hahahahaha... Bwahahahahaha!" The demon released a bloodcurdling laugh from its headless body. "I buried him in the ground. As for my objective, Master Zeleburg has ordered me to revive the Despair-Eating Dragon. This time, humanity will be exiled from the desert!"

"Hrm, thanks for being so chatty. And honest, at that." Alan's shovel could perform the functions of a lie detector, too. It even worked on demons.

"Hahahahahahaha! Foolish human, would you like to know why I'm being so honest with you?"

A rumbling noise filled the air. The demon's stomach split open, forming something shaped like a massive mouth. And within that mouth, intense flames began to flicker.

"It's because you all die here and now!"

"Alan, here it comes!"

"Fear not. I have a shovel." Alan knew that the demon was preparing to use its Fire Breath.

"Bwahahahaha! Ah, yes! The shovel can do anything and everything, is that right?"

"Seems like you're not convinced. I guess I'll just have to show you."

Alan summoned an aura of light blue energy, collecting it at the tip of his shovel. This was the Shovel Power that could bend space itself.

"DIG!"

His special Wave Motion Shovel Blast instantly fired off, causing the light blue aura to explode outward with an ear-splitting noise. The light radiating from it was like the sun itself. The demon's Fire Breath paled in comparison to the light of Alan's cannon. This shovel energy was capable of destroying all. It even rivaled the power of a small Big Bang.

It took three seconds for the light to fade.

"Shovels can dig up things and bury them. They can also..."

The demon had disappeared into the light. All that remained were the traces of Alan's beam on the scorched earth.

"Fire Wave Motion Shovel Blasts."

Silence settled upon the village.

Catria did everything in her power to resist the urge to comment. She knew better than to ruin the moment.

Julia, on the other hand, could do naught but stare. She couldn't wrap her head around what had just transpired. First, she'd thought that the elder had been murdered. Then, he'd been revealed to be an imposter. And now, he'd apparently been consumed and disintegrated by Alan's shovel.

"Julia, that was the most fundamental tenet of mining," Alan said.

"...Huh?"

"If you keep delving deep beneath the earth, you're sure to eventually encounter powerful obstacles. Impenetrable bedrock, a river of magma—you get the idea. That Doppelganger was your obstacle. Do you know what you're supposed to do when you run into something like that?"

She didn't know. She didn't understand any of what Alan did.

"It's when you come up against an obstacle like that when a shovel comes in handy. The most fundamental tenet of mining..."

Tears formed in Julia's eyes as it began to dawn on her.

Her heart had been wounded over and over again, and she truly had no idea what was going on. But there was one thing she knew beyond a shadow of doubt to be true, and it was that the man standing before her, shovel in hand...

"...is reducing all obstacles in your path to dust."

Was a man capable of reducing all common sense to dust.

▷━━━━━▶

That night, the villagers gathered in the center of the village. Among them was the village elder who the Doppelganger had replaced.

"I'm so sorry, Julia. I'm so, so sorry..."

He was alive and well. Well, technically he had died of suffocation after being buried by the Doppelganger, but thanks to Alan's shovel reversing the flow of the ground's time, he'd been returned to life. None of which made any sense.

"Didn't you say that you couldn't bring people back to life?"

"I can control the flow of time within the earth to a certain degree. If a person dies after being buried in the earth, there might be something I can do."

"Please leave the miracles to the gods..." Catria sighed.

Julia was performing the Ritual of Water Summoning in the center of the crowd. She was giving it everything she had, her wavy priestess' garments rippling through the air. But something was different from when she performed for the party in the carriage. In her right hand, she held a small blue shovel.

A dancing priestess complete with a shovel. Catria had a headache.

"Hey, Alan, what's up with that?"

"I powered her up."

"Wha?"

"By having the Water Priestess hold a water-colored shovel, her water summoning power was increased by 100 percent."

"Alan... Are you just making this up as you go?"

"I'm not lying."

The proof of the pudding was in the eating. Each time Julia stabbed her shovel into the ground, water began to gush from the hole with incredible force. The priestess was soon drenched, her outfit rendered see-through, laying her bountiful breasts bare for all to see. In the midst of all of this, the girl had a bright smile on her face.

She held her shovel like a precious treasure, rubbing her cheek against it. Julia clasped the shovel to her large breasts and held it tight.

"Ah, Sir Alan..." She was crying, but they were tears of joy this time.

"See? It worked."

Catria sighed deeply. Julia and her village were saved. How could she complain?

"By the way, where did Her Royal Highness get off to?" The knight hadn't seen her for a while now. Despite so many being present for this display of shovel power, she was nowhere to be found. Normally, she'd be overcome with rabid joy by now.

"She said she had something to prepare with Alice."

Just then, an unfamiliar voice called his name. Alan turned around to see the villagers clustering around some kind of object, chanting as they did.

Lithisia, Alice, and tens of villagers were facing it.

"The Rahal Tribe has been saved! This is all thanks to the power of the shovel!"

"Shovel! Alan! Shovel! Alan!" chanted the villagers. They were all holding shovels that they'd taken from their homes. The object they were gathered around, being led in their chanting by Lithisia, was none other than a copper statue of Alan himself.

"Let us all follow in the Water Priestess' example! Let us all become children of the shovel!"

"Sh-shovel! Shovel! We must all shovel together!"

Even Alice was cooperating. Lithisia had probably threatened her.

"Shovel! Shovel! Shovel!" The chanting grew fiercer.

"We are all one people! One people who have gazed upon the miracle of the shovel!" delivered Lithisia, with a radiant smile on her face.

Catria whispered in Alan's ear. "Er, shouldn't we be stopping her?"

"How exactly would you propose we do that?"

"All hail the shovel!"

Catria shook her head at him. "I have no clue."

The chanting continued in harmony.

That day, the oasis was returned to life and the Holy Shovel Faith gained 58 new believers.

Princess Lithisia was only just getting started.

The next morning, once the excitement had died down, Alan and the others finally managed to get some information about the Red Orb from the village elder.

The Doppelganger had placed it deep below the pyramid. Julia would serve as their guide.

"It's a very old structure, so there are traps everywhere. Even thieves and adventurers dare not come near."

"Don't worry, I've got this." Alan gripped his shovel. "Shovels were made to dig things up."

That might be the first logical thing he's ever said, Catria thought to herself.

THE INVINCIBLE SHOVEL

PART 15
The Miner and the Mystery of the Pyramid

THE BLINDING LIGHT of the sun illuminated the desert. Alan paved a road made of marble through the sand with his shovel while the rest of the party followed in the carriage.

As they traveled, Julia began to speak of a local legend. According to her, the pyramid they were headed to had been built to imprison an ancient dragon.

"Over 300 years ago, this used to be grassland. Then a Divine Dragon with wings massive enough to block out the sun emerged from the depths of hell and laid waste to the earth with its fire breath, completely incinerating the grasslands. This is the Legend of Rahal."

"Hrm, and you're saying that dragon sleeps within the pyramid?"

Julia nodded her head. "I...believe it's really there." When she first approached the pyramid as the chosen sacrifice, she'd heard its voice. The ancient dragon had filled the young girl with incomprehensible terror, despite only being a voice in the wind.

"Are you sure you want to do this?"

"Yes, I am. When the dragon appears, I must be present."

Julia's Ritual of Water Summoning had originally been a technique to create a water barrier that could defend against the dragon's fire breath. She was certain the party would need her assistance.

The girl gripped her blue shovel.

"I... I can't stop shaking, but..." She had to do what she had to do. Alan had saved both her and her people. He had saved everything that meant anything to her. "I have to be brave. I'm going to fight alongside you."

"...Well, just don't push yourself too hard. Hey, Catria?"

"What?"

"We're not prioritizing safety first this time. We're going to do things the normal way."

"Huh, fine with me... Wait, wait! You're not fooling me!" Catria knew that Alan's "normal" couldn't possibly be the same as hers.

"No, seriously. I want this to be a mission that any of us could complete on our own. When we conquered Riften,

I realized something. Shovel rookies can't create Shovel Soldiers or put up barriers around a dungeon."

"Shouldn't that have been the first thing you realized?"

"And so, I thought to myself: we still have five orbs left, right? It's entirely possible that in the future, we'll be acting separately and will have to traverse dungeons on our own. And if that's the case, I want to teach you how to handle one with techniques that are within your grasp."

"Hrm, i-is that so...? Huh." Catria couldn't say she was opposed to the idea. There was something terribly heroic and almost romantic about exploring a pyramid in search of a legendary orb. "Okay, fine. So what's the deal?"

Once he and Catria had come to an agreement, Alan remounted the carriage. Inside, Lithisia had a scroll open on the floor and was in the process of jotting something down. Next to her, Alice was drawing a picture.

"I'll have you know, I've only ever drawn for Father!"

"Don't worry! You're way more talented than me! Good luck!"

"...What are you two doing?"

"Ah, Sir Miner! Heh heh, well, you see..." Lithisia wore the smile of a young, embarrassed maiden. "Alice and I are shoveling down the Shovel Faith scripture!"

Well then.

"...Oh." Alan had given up. All he could do was let out a deep sigh, leaving her to her madness. But then, Lithisia's expression suddenly changed.

"Um." She gazed at Alan, looking concerned. "E-excuse me... Um, Sir Miner? Are you perhaps displeased with the scripture?"

"Hm."

"Er, if you are, I, well..."

This was his chance. He could finally tell her how he truly felt about all of this madness. But as he looked at the princess, Alan hesitated. She was staring at him with the gentle eyes of a fifteen-year-old girl. There was no sign of her usual stubbornness. If he told her to nix all this religion stuff, she probably would. But was that the right move?

At the end of the day, Lithisia always looked like she was having the time of her life whenever she spoke of shovels. Could Alan really take that joy away from her?

"Sir Miner..." Lithisia waited quietly for his response, as if she were praying.

Alan was incapable of willingly plunging this young girl into the depths of despair. *It's not like she's hurting anyone.* Sure, the future of Rostir, no, the continent, was up in the air, but as long as he made sure she didn't do anything irreversible, what harm was there in letting her be?

And so, Alan placed his hand on her head and gently patted it. "Don't give me that look. I don't mind."

Lithisia's smile returned in a flash. "R-really?!"

She looked like a young child. It was enough to put a smile on even Alan's mug. "But, well, let me say this much. Try to keep the weird shovelisms to a minimum, okay?"

"Oh my gosh! I'm so so sorry for being a weird shovelism princess! Um, could it be that I don't quite understand the meaning of shoveling the way I thought I did?"

"If anything, you've gone far past its original meaning."

"I-In that case..." Lithisia covered her mouth with her shovel, her cheeks bright red with embarrassment. "Um, after we find the orb, if it's okay with you... c-could you teach me how to shovel properly one more time...?"

A few seconds of silence followed. Quite frankly, Alan didn't really understand where Lithisia was coming from, but he did recognize that he was the root of the issue. It was his responsibility to see this through to the end. And so, he replied, "Sure. Once we get out of Desertopia, I'll put your nose to the grindstone."

"Grind?! Oh gosh..."

Lithisia shivered. Her body was trembling. She bowed her head repeatedly to Alan as tears ran down her cheeks. "Thank you so much! I'm shovely happy...!"

"I get the feeling this sickness of hers is only going to get worse...." Alice sighed.

"Alan, the pyramid is in sight," Catria yelled from outside.

The miner gripped his shovel. "Watch carefully, Catria. As long as one has a shovel, anyone can delve deep within ruins."

The knight felt a cold bead of sweat run down her back. Somehow, she had a bad feeling about those words of his.

⊳────────▶

The first obstacle was the entrance. The pyramid had no door to speak of—each side of the building was a flat wall with no way to get in.

"'Call upon the name of our ancient enemy, lest the way remain closed.' That's what the legend says," Julia offered.

"So it's a riddle!" Catria was fascinated. A secret password to open a secret door! This was a true adventure.

"Hrm, a riddle, eh? Time to bust the old shovel out." Alan used his shovel to write "name of our ancient enemy" into the sand. He then scooped that sand aside to reveal a stone underneath, with the word "Glaurung" carved into it. The second Alan said that name out loud, a part of the pyramid's wall slid to the side.

A hidden passage.

"Hey..." Catria's voice issued from the very pit of her stomach.

"You dig out the truth. This is one shovel technique that anyone can use." *If they're a shovel user, that is.* "This is one of the basics. Don't tell me you can't do it?"

"Of course I can't!"

"Catria, don't say that until you've at least tried. C'mon. Give it a shot."

"It's impossible! I'm just an ordinary person! I'm not even like the princess!"

"C-can we maybe get a move on...?"

Julia's timid plea spurred them to continue. But the path ahead was dark, dank, and narrow, and the only source of illumination was the light coming off the tip of Alan's shovel.

"Shovel Light. Dungeons are dark places, so you need light to scare off the terrors lurking within."

"The fact that this doesn't even surprise me anymore makes me fear for my future."

Thanks to Julia's knowledge of the old legends, the party had a fair idea of where they were headed. After proceeding into the depths of the pyramid for a while, they hit a dead end with five buttons embedded in the wall. Next to the buttons were directions written in an ancient language. This was clearly the key to solving yet another puzzle.

"Are you going to dig up the truth with your shovel again?"

"No. I don't need to. This is much simpler." Alan quickly used the blade of his shovel to pry the buttons free of the wall. Attached to the back of each button was a series of wires woven together in a complex fashion. "I'm going to analyze how this is all wired together."

The light in Catria's eyes vanished.

"There are physical lines and magical lines. Regardless of which one you're dealing with, your shovel can make hidden wiring visible. In this case, the wiring going up into the ceiling and the floor connects to traps, so the middle button is the correct answer."

Could this even be described as dungeon delving anymore?

"Whew, this one was really simple. Catria, as long as you have a shovel on you, you can do this."

"No, I can't!"

"Catria, give it a try. That's an order."

"URGH!"

Catria couldn't object. She'd vowed to be Lithisia's loyal servant until the day she died. And so, dejected, she poked at the wall with her shovel.

But then...

The image of all five buttons and their wiring appeared in her mind, clear as day.

"WHAAAAAAA?!" She'd actually done it. Had she already been that contaminated by this shovel nonsense?!

"Catria, remember. You're a wielder of the Holy Knight Shovel."

"I'm so proud of you! I always believed in you!"

"No, no, no! This is madness! I'm a swordswoman, not a shovel user!"

"You're both! You're a Shovel Knight!"

"Can we *please* hurry up?!"

With the correct button pressed, the party proceeded forward. Using Alan's shovel to guide them, they made a beeline straight for the innermost sanctum of the pyramid. Erected in the midst of an otherwise open space stood an ancient, elaborately carved door, guarded by a statue of a sphinx.

"Intruder, I have a question to ask of you." A bestial voice echoed throughout the room.

"Another riddle... You gonna dig this one up with your shovel?"

"No. The sphinx statue is judging this one. If we solve this the wrong way, it'll attack."

"You mean you can't just shovel your way out of everything?!"

"Hush. Here comes the riddle. Make sure you listen carefully."

"It has four legs in the morn, two in the day, and three at night. What is it?"

"Hold up. Even I know this one." Just as the gears in Catria's head began to turn...

"A shovel!" Lithisia shouted. "I mean, the shovel I saw in my dream this morning crawled on four legs. As for during the day, well, Alan's Shovel Soldiers have two legs! And then at night, well, it's too embarrassing for me to say out loud, but..." Lithisia's cheeks grew pink. "Anyway! The answer is 'shovel'! I know I'm not wrong!"

The sphinx was silent. Despite being a stone statue, it was...sweating?! It almost looked like it was emitting a silent cry for help.

"...You mean she's not wrong?" Catria whispered, once she'd finally regained consciousness (after blacking out for a moment).

"There is more than one possible answer to the riddle. As long as the guardian accepts the answer, we're good to go."

"You're telling me it accepted 'shovel' as a proper answer...?"

"It kind of made sense."

"In what world?!"

The sphinx was sweating bullets at this point. At long last, it managed to form words. "...Human... The shovel you speak of... Is it not a human being?"

It's checking her answer?!

"I suppose you could say it is. The very concept of humanity is contained within the notion of the shovel, after all!"

"...In other words, one might say your answer is... a 'human'?"

"No, I'd say my answer is 'shovel.'"

...

"The answer is 'shovel.'"

Lithisia sounded perfectly confident. Meanwhile, the sphinx statue began to tremble minutely. *Someone, anyone, please save me,* said the look on its face. Eventually, it spoke again.

"I accept defeat."

A baritone rumbling filled the air as the statue hastily withdrew back into the wall, and the magnificently carved door creaked open. Lithisia held up her shovel victoriously. "I did it! I won, Sir Miner!"

Indeed, her shovel had defeated the riddle. Somehow. "I had no idea a shovel could be used like that. Amazing work, Lithisia."

"Amazing?! O-oh my gosh…"

"Catria, do you think you can learn that technique?"

"I don't think anyone but the princess could ever pull that off." There was nothing for Catria to learn from this dungeon run. "Anyway, where's the orb? Is that it?"

"Y-yes, it should be sitting right on the… Huh?!"

Julia immediately went tense all over. The Red Orb was indeed sitting in the center of the vault, but it was bathed in a dark miasma. The room was glowing with immense heat, as if it were filled with magma. And then, the very next instant—

ROOOOOOOOOAAAAAAAAAAR!!!

A terrible, soul-rending howl filled the room. Alan quickly jumped in front of the girl and slashed his shovel through the air. The sheer force of the sound wave was deflected by his tool, but the words made their way through nonetheless.

"I have attained the power of the treasure and awakened."

The roar was powerful enough to shake the very foundations of the world. And it was unmistakably the language of dragons.

It was then that the pyramid split.

Alan immediately threw up a shield barrier. Everything within the barrier was protected from all harm, but whatever existed outside of it was destroyed by the sheer power of the creature's roar. Stones flurried through the air like a kind of storm. Mighty sound waves crashed into equally intense heat waves, turning the environment outside the shield barrier into the very picture of hell.

This was nothing, however, compared to the overwhelming presence above them. Alan and the party all looked up at once. The pyramid was long gone, but the sky was still obscured from sight. Why?

Because colossal red wings had filled the entirety of their field of vision.

"That's a real dragon?!" Catria cried out.

"?!" Julia was frozen in fear. This was just like the first time she'd arrived at the entrance of the pyramid, alone, to sacrifice herself. This was the voice she'd heard. The voice that caused her to collapse in fear, be overcome by despair, and abandon all her responsibilities in order to flee.

But this time—

I... I...!

Julia gripped her blue shovel. It was time to repay Alan for all that he had done for her.

"Sir Alan! Allow me!" she said, and stepped in front of the miner.

"NNNAAAROOOAAAAAAAAR!!!"

The creature inhaled deeply, preparing to unleash its deadly fire breath upon the party. It was unmistakably a real, true dragon. All of the hairs on Julia's body stood on end. Her mind was a disordered mess. She was terrified. She didn't want to be here. She wanted to run.

But with one clang of her shovel, Julia banished all of those thoughts.

"Sir Alan! ALAN! ALAN!!"

Within Julia's eyes was the shining light of courage. In her left hand, she held a shovel. In her right hand, she grasped the edge of her robe. She began to dance with all the grace and elegance expected of a priestess. She was scared, and she was terrified, but she buried those feelings with her shovel and danced like her life depended on it.

A high-pitched sound rang through the air as a thick, blue wall shielded Alan and the others. This was the Rahal Tribe's secret technique, originally designed to protect against the dragon's breath—the Water Wall.

"I did it...!" Julia had finally repaid her debt to Alan! But just as she started to smile—

"Quite the annoyance." The dragon whipped its head. ZAP! And just like that, Julia's Water Wall vanished.

"What?!"

"Magic Erasure, eh?" Alan said, calmly assessing the situation. Elder dragons possessed magical powers far beyond that of any human. They could eliminate a barrier with a single breath.

"Fool. What an ignorant, powerless, pitiful insect you are." The dragon's voice rang directly in their minds. Julia was frozen still. She'd thought she'd finally made herself useful, but now, she understood she was in way over her head.

"Ah... Ahhh..." Tears began to fall from her eyes to the ground. Tears of despair.

"Death is all that awaits you, pitiful insect."

The beast unleashed its scorching hot breath in a flash of blinding light. Julia stood still. She was overwhelmed. The dragon was right; she was just a pitiful insect, and she was going to die here without a hope of fighting back. Humanity could never hope to defeat a creature like this. It had the power to rule the world.

But just then—

"Well done, Julia."

Alan made his move.

"DIG!"

A flash of light burst from the head of his shovel. The legendary dragon's torrent of fire was deflected ever so slightly to the side, almost as if it had intentionally missed Alan and the others. It spilled into the desert sands instead, immolating everything it touched.

Alan and Julia were unscathed.

"Dimensional Shoveling."

By shoveling the very matter of space itself, Alan was able to create a dimensional rift that affected the breath's vector, thereby changing its trajectory. It was an anti-dragon-breath technique that he'd developed specifically to deal with elder dragons. And since it wasn't magical in nature , the dragon's Magic Erasure ability was ineffective against it.

"Huh...?" Julia's jaw was on the floor. Alan flashed her a smile.

"It was thanks to you that I discovered one of its abilities."

"Wait, what?"

"You did well to not succumb to fear."

Julia looked up at Alan with tears in her eyes. In that moment, he seemed to her to be just as mighty—no, mightier even—than the dragon.

"You can leave the rest to me." Alan gripped his shovel. "Just give me three minutes."

"Sir Miner and his patented threshovdragking!" (Three-minute shovel dragon cooking!)

"That is definitely not a word."

"You dare raise your weapon against me?" The dragon lowered its gaze toward the miner, releasing a growl that sounded like a guttural chuckle. "Foolish man. Humans cannot hope to stand against my kind. That is the law of this world."

Alan grinned in response. "You're right. Men cannot defeat dragons. However...there are exceptions."

"What?"

KA-CHOOM!

A blue aura began to surround Alan's shovel.

"One only need to turn the tide with a shovel."

Alan was accumulating Shovel Power, building it up to hitherto unseen levels of intensity. The dragon's eyes glowed with sudden caution at this strange aura, which even it did not recognize. "What is that?"

"My shovel. It can pierce everything that ever has been or will be. Including—"

The tip of the shovel began to glow. This was the same light by which the miner had dug his way through the underworld.

"Even gods and dragons," Alan stated with determination.

PART 16

The Miner Defeats the Legendary Dragon

ALAN LEAPT into the sky.

That was right.

The sky.

The pyramid had collapsed, leaving only sky above the party's heads. It was this very sky that now served as Alan and the dragon's arena. The miner soared through the air, buoyed up by a circular field of blue light that emanated from his shovel. It looked less like he was flying, and more like he was simply leaping a distance no human could hope to match. He was like a Pegasus. A pegashovel.

"He told me he could do this, but actually seeing it with my own two eyes... well." What else could Catria say in response to such an insane sight?

"I always thought shovels were tools for digging through the ground."

"Julia, you're absolutely right. But the opposite is also shovely true."

"The opposite?"

"The opposite of digging through the ground is flying through the sky!"

"Are you sure that's what 'opposite' means?"

"Shovely so!"

"O-okay."

"Lithisia's confusing the Water Priestess. Do something, Catria." Alice turned to the knight.

Catria wished she could, but she was powerless here. Alan was flying. What could she possibly say in the face of that? The man with the shovel was using its bizarre powers to fly through the sky. Come on.

"How can a mere mortal fly through my dominion?! My sky?!"

"I'd be a terrible miner if I couldn't manage a little aerial combat."

There were elder dragons and higher demons that could eradicate the ground at a molecular level, create huge open-air cavities, shift into astral bodies and fly unrestricted through solid earth, or even create parallel dimensions advantageous to themselves. Being able to do battle in the air was a necessary prerequisite for going up against enemies that could control the very nature of reality.

"You who violates my dominion with your presence! I sentence you to death!"

The dragon unleashed another roar of pure anger. Cracks began to appear in the air, and from them emerged a legion of smaller dragons.

Dragon-summoning magic.

"Eliminate him, my children!"

The army of dragons simultaneously unleashed their fire breath upon Alan. But it was too late.

"BURY!" A flash of light erupted from his shovel and created a shield around him. The fire attacks were absorbed into this energy shield.

"Oh my gosh! Catria, you absolutely have to learn how to do that! It's your responsibility as the head of the Holy Shovel Knights!"

"That's not happening unless I give up on being human."

"Then toss your humanity aside!"

"..." Catria's expression was the picture of the kind of despair that consumed a knight upon receiving an impossible order from their master.

Alan's mid-air battle continued. He had already finished off the smaller dragons.

"Why doesn't Sir Miner end things with his Wave Motion Shovel Blast?"

"He's probably trying to get a read on the dragon's true power. Remember all that stuff about safety first?"

"Sir Alan..." Julia was on both knees, praying for his victory. In the face of such an inhuman battle, all mortals could do was prostrate themselves before a higher power.

"My powerful children! My brood! Assemble!" The dragon roared yet again, preparing to use more summoning magic.

"Like I'm going to let you." Alan lifted his shovel toward the heavens and focused his energy into it. *KA-CHOOOOOOOOOOM*! A howl erupted from the shovel that was not at all unlike the dragon's. Shockingly, this one was much louder. The dragon's summoning magic was overwritten, and the cracks in dimensional space closed.

"What was that?" Catria whispered. The shovel had howled?!

Off to her side, she could hear Lithisia hit upon a new, unsavory idea. "I get it! I totally get it! I finally understand, Sir Miner!"

"Your Royal Highness? What do you mean?" Catria didn't actually want to know.

"Listen shovely closely, Catria."

"I'm just going to ignore the 'shovely' part."

"Shovels are objects that 'dig up' things, correct?"

"Well, er, yes. Generally speaking. Though as of late, I've come to doubt that concept."

Lithisia held her index finger up. "Well, dogs dig up things as well! And they howl! See? It makes perfect sense for a shovel to do the same."

A strangely chilly breeze blew through the desert.

Lithisia continued with her explanation. "Sir Miner looked to Mother Nature for inspiration... How beautiful!"

"Going by that attempt at logic, you might as well start calling ice cream shops 'shovels', since there's so much scooping!"

"Oh my gosh! You're right! Let's do that when we take my country back!"

"I was a fool for saying anything."

And just like that, Rostir earned a new tourist attraction.

The battle waged on. Alan's shovel pierced the magically enforced scales of the dragon, which began to crack like dropped plates. On the surface, dragon scales were considered the hardest material in the world. That said, shovels were considered harder than all others beneath the surface.

"Dragon, it appears to me that your knowledge stops at the surface." Alan was beginning to grasp this beast's abilities. The dragon was undoubtedly strong. Its ability to summon its brood and the power of its fire breath placed it solidly among the most powerful members of its kind. And yet, compared to Alan, who had spent a thousand years digging beneath the surface, it showed an overwhelming lack of experience.

"Why?! How is this possible?! This is madness!" The dragon opened its maw, guided by its rage. It was planning on firing off its breath again.

Alan chose not to dodge. Now that he knew the limits of the beast's strength, he had no need to play it safe. He began to collect blue energy at the tip of his shovel.

Both combatants fired their attacks in the same moment, and the Wave Beam Cannon proved significantly more powerful.

"DIG!"

The Wave Motion Shovel Blast engulfed the dragon's breath, and the resulting collision tore open a rift in space. The ergosphere that formed around this void spun faster than light itself, radiating destruction in its wake. Gravity distorted. The laws of physics began to warp.

The planet, unable to withstand the immense power of the Wave Beam Cannon, was on the verge of collapse. It was a Shoveltastrophe.

And the dragon's massive body was being torn apart by the dimensional collapse.

"Why..."

Having recognized its own defeat, the ancient beast managed only that one word. Why? Why did it lose? *How* did it lose to a human?

"Dragon, there is but a single reason why you lost this battle. To put it simply... Dragon, your claws are incapable of holding a shovel."

The dragon let loose one final roar as its form was erased from existence. "I DON'T GET IT!" it cried.

Catria understood exactly where it was coming from. *Yeah, I know. I totally agree.*

And so, Alan returned to the surface with the Red Orb in hand. "Sorry to keep you waiting."

The first person to run up to him was Lithisia. "I'm so very moved! I must record today's battle in our scripture!"

"And how exactly do you plan on describing it?" asked Alice.

"Just say the shovel was victorious..."

"A perfect idea," responded the undead queen.

Leaving Alice and the others to figure this out, Alan approached Julia.

"The dragon... It's..." Julia was still staring slack-jawed at the demolished pyramid.

This was no longer a forbidden land, but rather, the grave of the Despair-Eating Dragon.

"Sir Alan, no, I mean, I... Ahhh..." Julia fell to her knees as if she were begging for forgiveness. "I can't believe I had the nerve to call you by your name! I..." Tears fell from the girl's eyes. "Someone like me... I... I should be calling you God!"

"C'mon, raise your head, Julia. I'm no god."

"B-but..."

Indeed, when it came to shovels, Alan was the man. But he didn't have the power to govern the world like a god, nor did he plan on becoming one.

"I'm Alan."

And so, he took a knee and looked Julia straight in the eyes.

"Just an ordinary miner."

A warm gust of wind blew through the desert. Julia simply stared into Alan's eyes. Who could blame her? She'd just heard the most incomprehensible words imaginable.

Eventually, someone patted Alan on the back. It was Catria.

"Alan, there's something I have to say."

"What is it?"

Catria sighed deeply. She had reached her limit. What she had to say next, she was saying on behalf of the rest of humanity—on behalf of the dead dragon, even. And so, she inhaled and then shouted with all of her might.

"HOW IN THE WORLD ARE YOU JUST AN ORDINARY MINER?!"

Her words echoed through the furthest reaches of the desert.

THE INVINCIBLE SHOVEL

Julia's Hot Spring Shovel (Preview Version)

LATER THAT NIGHT, Alan sat alone in a hot spring located in Rahal Village. The village elder had broken down in grateful tears upon being informed of the dragon's demise, and begged Alan to stay at least one night so they might throw a festival in his honor. In the meantime, he'd implored, Alan could take a dip in the village's hot spring. The hot spring that had only just come into existence because, as it turned out, Julia's water summoning power was too strong.

Julia, the Hot Spring Priestess.

"That's three orbs down," Alan muttered to himself. "Four to go. I wonder if I'll be able to keep my promise to Lithisia..."

The next orb was apparently located in the neighboring country. Lithisia wanted to collect all seven orbs and then drive Zeleburg from her homeland, but whether they'd actually get that far... Well, Alan wasn't sure. He was confident he could recover the orbs, but also concerned that the Holy Shovel Faith was rapidly becoming the primary objective of their travels.

"...Well, I'm sure it'll be fine."

Once they made it back to Rostir, she'd probably return to normal. She was just getting overexcited by going on a journey like this for the first time. Probably.

As Alan continued to turn a blind eye to reality...

"E-excuse me..." The wooden door slid open.

When Alan turned around, he caught a glimpse of blue hair and white skin that glimmered beneath the moonlight. It was Julia, but that wasn't what surprised him. No, it was the fact that she had abandoned her flowy priestess garments in favor of wearing nothing at all.

She was naked.

"Er."

All she had on was a wooden wash tub and a white towel. The latter was caught on her bountiful breasts, but did little to hide them. Alan could see the trembling spots of pink hidden beneath the white towel. While her most delicate bits were covered, the priestess' current state was nothing if not dangerous.

"Whoa, hold on! Julia, this is the men's bath!" Alan was actually panicked. The naked priestess' current look was unutterably sexy, and his adamantine self-control was on the verge of cracking.

Julia herself seemed slightly embarrassed, her face a shade of pink. "I-I know that th-this is the m-men's bath..."

"You do?!"

"Um, um, I, er, excuse me!" Covering her breasts with one arm, she reached into the wash tub and took something out. It was an object that really didn't belong in the bath.

A blue shovel.

"I shall abide by the commands of the High Priestess of shovels, a-and shovel your back!"

Alan regretted everything.

I should have nipped Lithisia's shovel fanaticism in the bud when I had the chance!

Lithisia's First Shovel Present

ALAN AND LITHISIA went through the elven castle's storerooms, grabbing the metals and precious gems they'd need to help restore the Elf Woods.

"Whew! Amazing! Amazing, Sir Miner! These are all jewels?" Lithisia said, visibly moved. As royalty, she'd had plenty of jewels in her life, but the ones currently before her were far more exquisite than any she'd ever seen. They shone in every imaginable color, were shaped in every imaginable pattern of facets. She could have spent the rest of her life just staring at them.

"Ah, that one is the Necklace of the Billion-Colored Dragon. I found it on Layer #797." As Alan explained this, Lithisia stared fixedly at the necklace. "...Do you want it?"

"Shovel?!" Lithisia answered, as incomprehensibly as ever. Apparently, he was right on the mark.

"If you want it, you can have it."

"Huh? A-are you sure?!"

"Yeah. It's useless to me, but I bet it'd look great on you."

Lithisia was overcome with great joy for but a moment before she calmed down. "Useless to you, Sir Miner?"

"Hrm? Yeah. If I wore accessories like that, it'd just make it harder to do my work." Alan said as he handed her the necklace.

The Necklace of the Billion-Colored Dragon shone with a dazzling iridescence. Lithisia was filled with the desire to reach out and take it. It wasn't just the plethora of colors that tempted her so, but the fact that this was a present from Alan. Of course she wanted it.

But...

"N-no, I can't!" Lithisia pulled her hand back.

"Lithisia?"

"U-um, the necklace is a royal treasure! I can't take it!"

Of course, that was a lie. Her real reason for not accepting it...

I mean, I mean... It'll be harder to shovel...

She wanted a present from Alan. She really did. But she couldn't accept this. At the end of the day, Lithisia wasn't trying to become a princess who dripped with shining jewels. She wanted to become the miner's wife. She wanted to shine brightest when she was sinking her shovel into the earth.

"...I see." Alan took a moment to think, then nodded.

"I-I'm so sorry, and after you offered and everything..."

"I got it. Lithisia, hand me your shovel."

"Huh?"

KA-CHOOOOM! A scattering of light erupted from his shovel and wove through the necklace and Lithisia's red shovel. In just a few seconds, the jewel had been embedded into the red shovel.

"Huh?!" Lithisia looked at her (new) red shovel. It looked as cute as ever, but the metal tip now shone with a new, brighter iridescence. Just by gripping the handle, she could feel immense power building up inside of her. This was the power of the jewel—no, the power of a miner.

"I improved the cutting power of your shovel. This way, the jewel won't get in the way."

"Ah..." The logic didn't matter. Lithisia's eyes were filled with tears.

"Whoa, what's wrong?!"

"Thank you so much, Sir Miner. I... I...!" Lithisia wiped her tears and rose to her feet. She held her (new) red shovel tightly. "I'll do my best!"

"Huh?"

"I swear upon this shovel that I will become a princess suitable to wield it!"

Alan looked at the fierce light shining off of her shovel. *Become? You already* are *a Shovel Princess.*

📖 GLOSSARY ❸

(`・ω・´)
(Shovel Wave Motion Shovel Blast)

noun

① The emoji that represents someone firing the Wave Motion Shovel Blast.

② Both eyebrows are exquisite.

③ The round eyes are particularly charming.

④ The cheek brackets convey an impression of gentleness.

⑤ Truth be told, I originally wanted to use the ASCII art as-is (12 lines), but my editor got mad and told me, "Titles don't have line breaks!" And so, I ended up shortening the title by using a face emoji.

⑥ Thank you for reading all the way through to this glossary. It looks like there's gonna be a Volume 2, so I hope you stick with us!

HOLY SHOVEL EMPIRE, OFFICIAL DICTIONARY
(AUTHOR: LITHISIA), 7TH VERSION.

Afterword

HI, TSUCHISE HERE. Now that we've got the introductions out of the way, let me explain why I wrote this little novel.

I started writing because of *The Lord of the Rings*, so as you can imagine, I wanted to write classic fantasy. And so, after doing some digging into what fantasy fiction meant to me, I realized that the most recent thing I'd seen that gave me that "classic fantasy" feel was the SR outfit of a certain idol who likes to dig holes for herself.

And so I made said idol's item the shovel, the main theme of my novel.

Next up was the main protagonist. A true hero fit for a classic fantasy yarn. The first person to come to mind was a hero from my hometown of Kobe, Ichiro. He's the truest hero I know, and his existence in and of itself feels like pure fantasy.

This led me to making the protagonist a superhuman who could probably score five points just by pumping his fist into the air.

Next, of course, came the heroine.

To make a likeable heroine, I looked into what made female characters attractive in a fantasy setting. In one certain massive RPG series, that quality is represented via "charisma." I thought about what it means for someone to have lots of charisma, and after doing some research, landed on ecclesiastical figures. In other words, the best fantasy heroines are people with passionate religious beliefs.

Once I had the theme, protagonist, and heroine set, the last thing left to do was figure out a special move for my hero. While watching the Koshien baseball tournament that summer, I noticed some fans in the Alps seats were belting out a parody of the *Space Battleship Yamato* theme. You can't have the *Yamato* without the Wave Motion Blast, and you can't get more fantastical than a Wave Motion Blast that can obliterate anything and everything. Besides, we now live in an era where even holy blades can fire off beams. It made total sense that, since the shovel was stronger than a holy blade, it could fire off a stronger beam in the form of the Wave Motion Shovel Blast.

And so I made my protagonist a superhuman who wields a shovel, my heroine the priestess of a new faith, and the Wave Motion Shovel Blast the special weapon of choice in my old-school fantasy novel.

I'm sure it's rather difficult for you, my readers, to really think of this as old-school fantasy. But to me, it is. So if this book resonates with you even slightly, I'll be so very glad.

Last but not least, I'd like to express a few words of gratitude. First and foremost, to my head editor who has taken great care of me. To Hagure Yuuki for drawing my shoveltastic heroine and protagonist. And of course, to all the readers who gave me the encouragement and motivation to keep writing back in my web novel days. I'm eternally grateful to you all.

Catch you later, folks. Yasohachi Tsuchise, signing off.